Blind Perspective

KRISTYN A. WAGNER

authorHOUSE

AuthorHouse™
1663 Liberty Drive
Bloomington, IN 47403
www.authorhouse.com
Phone: 1-800-839-8640

This is a fictional novel based on real events in the life of Kristyn Wagner

© 2011 by Kristyn A. Wagner. All rights reserved.

No part of this book may be reproduced, stored in a retrieval system, or transmitted by any means without the written permission of the author.

First published by AuthorHouse   11/04/2011

ISBN: 978-1-4634-2675-0 (sc)
ISBN: 978-1-4634-2676-7 (ebk)

Library of Congress Control Number: 2011910526

Printed in the United States of America

Any people depicted in stock imagery provided by Thinkstock are models, and such images are being used for illustrative purposes only.
Certain stock imagery © Thinkstock.

This book is printed on acid-free paper.

Because of the dynamic nature of the Internet, any web addresses or links contained in this book may have changed since publication and may no longer be valid. The views expressed in this work are solely those of the author and do not necessarily reflect the views of the publisher, and the publisher hereby disclaims any responsibility for them.

To My loving family and friends that pulled me through, and to you for taking the time to read this story

Acknowledgements

This book could not have come to life without so many people. I would like to thank the following people for their contributions to this book:

To my mother, Karen Wagner, who read and re-read my writing before dreams of a book had even materialized.

To my father, Richard Wagner, who supported the idea of a book even though it was abstract territory.

To my brother, Ryan Wagner, for always encouraging me to follow my dreams but also bring me back to reality.

To my sister, Rachel Wagner, who reminds me everyday to be a child and enjoy every second.

To one of my best friends, Jessica Tombs, for always being there no matter the time or how much drool.

To my many friends who were there for me when I needed you: my real prom date, the grounder boys, my badminton partner, and all my girls who supported me.

To David Feltmate, my first editor who didn't laugh at my sentences that didn't make sense but fixed them and also provided me with writers' insight, which I lacked.

To Julia Kibble, the creative and talented photographer behind the cover picture.

To Dr. Rootman and his team, who have helped me in this journey.

The eye sees only what the mind is prepared to comprehend

—Robertson Davies

The Beginning

*I don't know much,
but I do know more than
I knew yesterday.*

We all think we're normal. Or at least we think we know what normal is. But truth be told, normal only relates to our immediate life and who we know. Normal isn't what we see in magazines, on the TV screen, or pasted all over media and our world as we know it. We think normal is what is closest to us, our friends, family, and who we see at school. All I know is that ten months ago I thought I was normal, and now, let's just say I'm not so 'normal' after all.

My life was great. I walked the halls of Billa-Aid High School like I owned the place. I thought I was 'it and a bit.' Now, don't get me wrong; I wasn't the most popular, but I was happy and comfortable with who I was and lived my life like that every day. After all, this was my last year of high school and I would make the most of it. I took almost everything in my life for granted; I mean, why wouldn't I? It was all I had ever known. I had a course load that I could dominate so my grades would be excellent for university. I was taking some business, science, math, and history just to keep my options open. My teachers knew who I was because of Carter, my academic genius brother who came before me. Sure they had high expectations for me, but I survived and I held up the family tradition. I wasn't reaching Carter's academic genius status but I was sustaining the grades I needed, so I would be able to get into any program I wanted.

It was university response time and I started hearing from Western, Laurier, Waterloo, Guelph, Simon Fraser, University of British Columbia, Brock, and every other school I thought to apply to. That's right, I was a completely clueless adolescent when it came to my future plans. I just wanted to live my life and see how it would end up . . . all this planning threw me off. I didn't want to be stuck in one repetitive occupation for the rest of my life. The problem with me wasn't that I wasn't motivated enough; it was that I couldn't narrow down my options. I wanted every future out there. Paramedic sounded fun, but so did teacher, doctor, businesswoman, marine biologist, actress, science research assistant, sports announcer, and every other job. They all appealed to me! I wanted to do it all and be it all. That's kind of the same way I treated my friends and family.

My friend Anabeth once referred to me as a 'friend whore.' Okay, I know a whore is a bad thing and not something you want to be known as, but what in the world is a friend whore? So I asked her to break it down for me. She said that having so many friends at one time made me a 'friend whore.' I could only stare at her in puzzlement.

'You have friends everywhere you go and you are just so nice to everybody that even people who don't know you and only see your actions want to be your friend and invite you to things, making you a friend whore. You steal all the friends out there for us lonely people.' Anabeth finished her spiel, 'It's a good thing, and it's just amazing to watch how people are all drawn to you. I like sticking with one or two friends I can really trust. You cannot possibly feel close to all of the different people who call you their friend. It seems like a lot of shallow surface relationships.'

Wow. I didn't really know how to respond to this, but then I thought about my life and I realized I did have a lot of friends. I mean, if I were to have my wedding I would have no idea who my bridesmaids would be, let alone who would be invited. I seemed to share little bits of myself with lots of different groups, but never trusted my whole self with just one person. Good thing I wanted my wedding at Leeds Castle; I'm sure that could fit quite a few of us! Leeds Castle was a gorgeous castle I had seen when I was younger and I couldn't seem to shake that beautiful image out of my head for my wedding. The castle was in England, which would pose some difficulties later since I lived in Canada.

When you're a child and everything you could ever imagine feels like it could come true, Leeds Castle was the perfect place for my wedding.

I sometimes still think like a naive child who believes that everything will always work out and nothing bad can ever happen. I like to hold on to the innocence of a child and push the thoughts that couldn't be perfect out of my head. In my mind I was still a child, playing princess in a world where everything worked out happily ever after.

I got to thinking about what Anabeth said, and I realized I wasn't a friend whore because I had multiple shallow relationships. I was a friend whore because I cared about everybody's story and genuinely listened to every single person no matter who they were. Plus the fact that I was busy 24/7 and joined every club and every team helped me meet people pretty fast. It just made it hard to stay in deep relationships and continue to be 'best' friends with all of them. I did have my close friends that I would tell most everything to and have fun just sitting around doing nothing with.

I think that when you call up a friend to do nothing, that is when you are truly friends on a new level—that and being able to fart in front of a friend or not be ridiculously polite, just being comfortable with yourself. Friends that you truly believe would be there for you no matter if you didn't shower that day are friends that mean so much more than words can explain. Those friends are very rare and should be cherished.

I had a tendency to not care about others' opinions of me, or maybe I just became so used to pleasing other people that others became comfortable around me. This allowed me to meet many people and begin those 'shallow' relationships.

I did maintain some shallow relationships, but I don't know if that was a bad thing; I just enjoyed being a part of something bigger than me. Joining every club and being able to smile and say hi to everybody was something I truly enjoyed! Those shallow smiles made me feel accepted and loved, and they made me feel like I belonged.

I was a member of almost every club at our school; I was co-president for two years in DECA (a business club, DECA stands for Developing Excellence, Celebrating Achievement); running an environment club; an arts and crafts creator; BIN (Bill Intramural Network) member; *Aid* Beat (our school newspaper) article writer; and I would help out wherever was needed. I even worked a job at the pool teaching children how to swim and lifeguarding. I was also a sports nut. That's where my real identity came in. When people talked about me they would say, 'Oh yeah, that Riley girl she does everything, and does it with a smile, but man, does she play sports.' Or at least that's the identity I wanted everybody to believe. I wanted to be known as the happy, positive, unbreakable athlete.

I was known as the most athletic child out of the three children in my family, and soon enough I wasn't just the athletic one to everybody else, I was 'the athletic one' to me. It was where I seemed to fit in and be noticed. So I had to continue with my athletic identity if I wanted to exist. I mean, sure, everybody else kind of tells you who you are, and that is one way our identities are made. The self-fulfilling prophecy is when others choose for us and we chase their beliefs in order to gain our identity. I just got lucky that somebody chose such good traits for me to build my identity on.

It was spring, and all the snow was melting away. People started busting out the shorts and their pasty white legs to go with them. School had a changing atmosphere. People were busy, and I mean *everybody*. There was a buzz in the halls. People would rush home just so they could go outside and throw a football around with some buddies or make some lemonade. The malls were packed with summer and spring clothes and winter jackets and skis were on sale at half price. Everybody could sense summer getting closer! My graduating class was receiving our university and college application responses and some kids were marking out their futures and picking schools. Kids were responding to their applications and then going out and buying dorm sheets to celebrate. Me, on the other hand, I was waiting for the very last minute. I had no idea and I felt that rushing the decision would just make it be the wrong one. Sure, it's a little bit frustrating when you turn on your computer and your Facebook home page is filled with 'Waterloo, here I come', 'Guelph, can't wait to get there', 'Laurier, you're officially mine!' 'Accepted to Waterloo? Really, I agreed before they changed their mind!' and other 'decision made' quotes that emphasize how you have very little time to decide the rest of your life. What did I do to distract myself from all the caving-in pressures of the world? Well, I did what I do best. I kept busy and pushed those worrisome thoughts out of my fairytale.

I was playing badminton with my partner Miles when I decided I would try out for rugby just because it was one sport I had never tried. The swim team was still practicing bright and early because, after all, we made it to CWOSSA, the regional competition. I had three school sports on the go and I still felt like I had lots of time to think about my crumbling future. I continued to play rep basketball, too.

My day would consist of waking up early, which consisted of going to the pool at such ridiculous hours that the sun even knows it's too early and hasn't come up yet; then I would rush to class for the morning; eat lunch with 'my grounder boys' and our friends (I'll explain them in a bit); help out with intramurals or run a DECA meeting or make a poster depending on the day; and finally go to class for a few more hours. This is where most peoples' day ends—they go home and throw that football around—but mine continued. I would then go to badminton practice with Miles before running over to rugby practice. Afterwards, I would go to the pool, teach swimming lessons for a bit, and then my mom would pick me up and I would eat dinner in the car on the way to basketball, where I would have a lovely hard-core practice that I never thought I would survive. When I realized I was still alive after practice, Dad would drive me home and I would do my homework until super late and then crash—also known as falling asleep—until I started it all over again the next day. Yes, that was my life. Or at least the actions that made up my life.

Maybe you are wondering why I hated my family so much and felt the need to hardly see them. Truth be told, I love every single one of my family members so much—even down to the dog. I have a mom who I would bond with in car rides and I tell her everything. She is a huge part of my life, but I definitely take her for granted as my taxi service. Sometimes I would be in such a rush I wouldn't even thank my mom or talk to her at all in the car because I was too busy stuffing my face with my dinner. I always expected Mom to be there for me, but I never realized what it would cost her. I shared a very similar, yet different, relationship with my dad. My dad, well I was Daddy's little girl and I loved him so much, even if we weren't all mushy gushy or showed our love through hugs and kisses. I just loved being with him. He worked as a professor at Laurier, ran his own business, and he still managed to come out and watch all of my sporting competitions and give me advice after each game on what I had to improve. We talked sports together, or about business and what to invest in, or about how school was going as we ate family dinners (which we normally ate together—especially on weekends, if we weren't all dispersed in our busy days).

Then I had a younger sister, Brianne. She was at high school with me and she was brilliant and gorgeous. My acquaintances at school, the guys I knew and would always smile at but generally would just continue walking by, would sometimes joke and ask me if three years was too big an age gap to date somebody—namely my sister. I just rolled my eyes and said that I would like to see that happen. Brianne was very independent and she didn't need a boy in her life to be who she was. She was smart and gorgeous and guys dreamed about being her boyfriend, but none of them dared to try. Brianne was like a little untouchable trophy that nobody could reach. Brianne and I were built-in best friends. We made a bond, pinkie promised and everything, that we would always be each other's best friend and nobody could come between us. Sure, she would steal my clothes and tell me I smelt bad, but we loved hanging out with one another. She was my little sister and I would do anything for her, even if it meant that when we were at the cottage I would sleep on the bad side of the bed, the side without the alarm clock.

My older brother, on the other hand, he was a genius. When I say genius I mean pure Einstein genius. He was expected to cure cancer or come up with the $E=MC^2$ of our time. Carter went to Waterloo for nanotechnology engineering and he lived at home. I would see glimpses of him and we would talk and catch up. He helped me with my homework and I would tell him about my life. He had the best girlfriend ever, but I'm pretty sure she liked him way more then he would ever like her. All I knew was she was a bombshell, prom queen in high school, at University of Waterloo for math, and a nice person to boot. Carter seemed to have all his ducks in a row, as some would say. He was super focused on school and it felt different having a part-time brother who would only tease you sometimes and be invisible or locked in his room studying the rest. Carter and I would have intense conversations about things only he and I would be comfortable talking about, and then we wouldn't talk to each other for a day or two except the occasional, 'Night, love you.' I would turn to Carter when I needed advice on my first kiss, which I had not had yet, and which seemed very scary. He was my older brother; he had all the answers, whereas Brianne was my best friend. She had no answers but was always there to hang out and have fun.

My family is the best and I love them, but everybody in my family has their identities and they were always busy running around doing something or another. Therefore, if I wanted to exist and have an identity of my own and not be invisible I had to be busy, too. I joined in the chaos and continued living my busy life.

We had all been placed in a different busy lifestyle. Before we all had our individual identities, our family would hang out all day. True, we still took a break from our busy lives to take family vacations together and we tried to get a family board game night in there, but as we got older our relationships started to change and we became individuals instead of one big family. I missed the times when we were all under the age of seven and my brother would put the pots and pans on both of our heads and my sister would bang on them in our own sibling band. Our family was now what I thought was a 'normal' family in today's world. We were a family where each member was valued and appreciated for his or her own individual identity.

So I was a pretty normal girl, if you asked me. I was one of the happiest girls around but it wasn't because of achievements or keeping too busy to feel the down side of life, it was because of my friends. I usually hung out with two boys, Dixon and Jonah. They were awesome and I loved them like brothers. I would play shot-for-shot with them and they wouldn't go easy on me; I actually got more than one bruise from this game with them. Shot-for-shot is when you each take turns punching the other person, getting increasingly harder to see who is the 'toughest.' They treated me like another boy. I'm pretty sure they called me an honorary boy so I could be included in 'boy's nights.' These boys were very childish and enjoyed going out and being active; they actually did things that were different from the gossip girls my age. My family called them the 'grounder boys', partly because they kept me grounded in my innocence and also because grounders was one of the many childish games we enjoyed playing together. Sure, I had lots of friends that were girls too, but I wasn't as close to them as I was with the boys. The best people in the world surrounded me, and the truth was I had no idea that these amazing people I talk about expanded beyond my grounder boys until one day in May.

My normal life changed in less than a blink of an eye. We have no control over some things, and these uncontrollable events can decide who we will become and what will happen in our life. But I did have control over one major decision in my life, and it was time to make it.

Future Plans

*The difference between good and
greatness is choices!
Make great choices and you will be great!*

It was getting close to crunch time. Not only were universities and colleges expecting answers back regarding my future, I also had to decide what I was going to do in the summer. It's hard enough trying to plan for the day, let alone the rest of your life. I really wanted my summer to be the best one ever, just in case I screwed up my future life with a bad university decision. I loved how when you were a part of so many teams and activities you didn't really need to plan at all. Practices were always scheduled for you and your life was pre-arranged with limited decisions that needed to be made. So I decided to apply to Muskoka Woods. I figured I would keep my options open. Plus my one friend Anabeth kept hammering it into my head, 'Oh, Riley, the boys are gorgeous and Christian. They are all athletic and super tanned. It's the perfect environment. You can find your future husband there. You'll love it! Please at least just apply—you can always say no.' Then she would show me these incredible movie clips of crazy sports like wakeboard flips and paintballing! It looked like a blast!

I applied to Muskoka Woods because, after all, I did want to find a husband. He would really help in my fairytale plan to have a wedding at Leeds Castle. Plus Anabeth showed me Facebook profiles of some of the people who worked there and they were gorgeous—so who wouldn't want a gorgeous husband? I was the kind of girl who dated boys because I was looking for a husband and somebody to build a life with, not just to fool around with, or waste time and get into trouble with. I wanted to find that Prince Charming, or at least learn what qualities I liked and disliked in a boy to help me find the man that would be my Prince Charming and be my future husband and father to my kids.

This decision about Muskoka Woods was a key asset in delaying my decision about which university to attend. I took all the time I needed to focus on this camp decision so my mind would be distracted from the dawning university decision. Muskoka Woods seemed perfect for me. Sports, boys, a chance to hang out and influence some kids' lives – I was set! I loved the idea of helping a child grow.

Even when you teach a child swimming lessons one night a week for only a few months of their lives you can teach them something they'll keep forever. Maybe it's how to do a front float, back swim, or silly side floats that are super hard and strange, or maybe it's something like saying please and thank you that will stick with them forever. So I applied to Muskoka Woods and I crossed my fingers for the chance to get hired and have the opportunity to have the best summer ever. Then I moved on to some other decisions.

Badminton season was quickly coming to an end for most of the team. Miles and I competed at the Waterloo County Secondary School Athletic Association (WCSSAA), which is the first of many serious competitions. We played well in the round robin and made it to the finals without any problems. Then we faced Northview. Northview School had the best coaches around; they were on their game, and we were flustered. The stands were packed and our coaches were nowhere to be found. Miles just grabbed my shoulders and said, 'Riley, we move on no matter what, but I want us to focus; we can do this, we can win and get the gold.' So Miles and I played with intense passion, but something wasn't in our game. Miles had been up all night the night before working on his co-presidential campaign and doing a calculus assignment. I was crashing because of how busy I was. We were both mere centimeters away from where we needed to be on every shot. We ended up taking the match to three games before we came up short, this time not by centimeters, but by three points. It was a close game, but Miles and I were ultimately disappointed.

The Northview fans cheered and our fans left with their heads hung in shame. Miles and I gave each other a nice sweaty hug and then started undoing our laces because we had to accept defeat. We knew we would get another chance to take this team down, and we would hopefully continue on after our next tournament.

The following day at school Miles showed the school his campaign video and it was a huge hit! The whole school was on board with 'Miles the Man'. I was so happy to have him as a badminton partner. I never really saw Miles as much other than his twin sister's brother before I started playing badminton with him. But then when we played together it was so easy, so right. I wanted to make him proud, and yet I could totally be myself. He was the perfect friend—pushing me to be the best I could be, but still allowing me to be myself and set my own goals. If I couldn't reach a shot, he would be there. We had excellent chemistry, just not on the night of WCSSAA finals. I was going through a whole stream of different events every day, but badminton was the activity that mattered the most.

Once my coach told me that it took a true athlete to play badminton. Certain sports required skill, others required the ability to jump or run and others were based on emotional and mental capacity to succeed but badminton took all elements of sport and put them together. Badminton was the sport that would demonstrate a true athlete, somebody who would be able to learn or pick up the other sports easily. She told me that badminton could not be practiced and perfected; it took true natural talent as well as hard work.

This made me believe that if I could succeed at badminton, maybe I would be able to play sports in university. These matches and games would end up deciding my future for me. Miles and I were just tired, and our heart and love of the game wasn't enough to pull us through. At least, not enough this time.

Identity

> *Find out who you are,*
> *then start being her*
> *on purpose.*
>
> —Dolly Parton

We continued to train, and I mean *train*. Miles played softball as well as continuing to campaign for co-pres. Luckily, swimming had finished for me. I was playing rugby and we had started outdoor practices, so I was going from rugby practice right after school to badminton practice to work teaching swimming lessons, then basketball practice. Our training for badminton was so intense and hard-core we brought in alumni that had been to provincials in previous years. We worked hard, but somehow it was still fun. Miles seemed a little unfocused, though, and it was hard when he was dealing with all the stress of the co-pres campaign as well. When Miles wasn't 100 percent focused, I didn't feel like I was either. I would sometimes just practice half-heartedly. Badminton really was a team sport, and if one of us was off our game, the other person suffered and lost motivation as well.

Northview Secondary School invited us for a 'practice' at their school. I'm pretty sure the coach just wanted to scout us out and pick up on our weaknesses. He asked Miles and I personally, and then he later invited the rest of our teammates who were moving on. Miles and I wanted our redemption, even if it meant sacrificing our strategy.

We arrived at Northview and all the nets were set up. Their professional coach was there and he welcomed us right away and set up a game. Miles and I were smacking the birdie around for a bit, just warming up. Then we were ready. We got our chance to beat them and redeem ourselves. We started playing and the Northview coach continued coaching his team, but not Miles or I. Our coaches had stayed back at our high school to coach the rest of the team.

Then Brodie, the other singles player who came along, was like, 'Hey, can you coach us too so it's a productive practice for us both?' The coach was like, 'Yeah, no problem, man?' The Northview coach was able to coach us on individual skills, but he never gave away any of his team's weaknesses. We were able to cream the Northview team. We were on our game, and it wasn't even close. As a bonus, we learned from the hints he told us so our game only got stronger.

Central Western Ontario Secondary School Association (CWOSSA) was approaching and Miles's campaign was coming to an end. We would find out who our co-pres was the day before CWOSSA. It put enormous pressure on the vote, not only for the future of the school, but also for the future of our badminton career. Emotions play a huge part in sports, and the campaign would play a huge part in our CWOSSA experience. My volleyball coach once told me that sports were 80 percent mental and only 20 percent physical. This meant that the vote deciding our school's fate would most likely be able to make or break our fate in badminton as well.

At this point Miles had to quit the softball team, but I was still doing double practices. I had to be very careful, though, because rugby was a dangerous sport and I was a flank/lock, which meant I was in the middle of the tackles. I was also thrown in the air on lineouts and they toss the ball right down the shoot, which is a line of people holding other teammates up in the air. My job was to fight with a girl in the air to try and get the ball. I loved rugby, but it also jeopardized my health. My parents were terrified of me playing and they didn't want to encourage it, although once I made my decision to play they supported it and bought me a scrumcap to protect myself.

Wednesday night was game night for rugby, so we had to practice super late for badminton. It was the last game before CWOSSA badminton. Our rugby match was against Lawn Weber at home. It was so intense and the weather conditions were brutal. It was also the first game Dad had come out to watch. The score was zero-zero after the first half.

I had played the whole first half and was covered in mud and some blood. The field was ripped apart. Tackles were crazy; people got rocked right into puddles.

The second half was starting and the crowd could feel the tension, despite the fact that most people had resorted to watching the game from their cars because the rain was horrendous! My grounder boys were in my car watching with my parents. I was so excited they had finally come out to watch a game. They always chirped me at lunches because it was my first year playing and the first game of the season I didn't get any minutes. I had been known as the 'bench warmer', and I had to erase that title. I had proved to them that I was playing, and I even got to start. I knew they would think that it was just luck if I didn't do something spectacular. I had to prove myself and my title as an 'athlete' and not just a duster on the sidelines.

Number eight from Lawn Weber had the ball and started running on the far wing. I knew this was my chance—I could reach her and bring her down! So I ran as hard as I could and dove to reach the tackle. I felt my arms wrap her legs and bring her down. This girl was huge and she landed on my head and I kind of just crunched under her weight. The ball came loose from her grip and I maintained possession as I was being crunched. The ref came and blew the whistle. Number eight stood up and I just lay there. My coach (a retired police officer who scared me so much at the beginning of the season—but I couldn't help but love him after the first game) came running towards me. I slowly got up and looked around. Coach asked me a few questions and brought me to the sidelines as the game progressed. My parents and the boys came over to see if I was okay. I told them that I was fine and needed to get back into the game. There were only ten minutes left and it was still scoreless. I looked at my parents and Mom asked if I was actually okay. I told her I was and Coach subbed me back in the action. Dad, in utter shock of the intensity and severity of the game, retired to the car to watch the last few minutes.

I got subbed in on the lineout and snatched the ball from the other team and outputted it to Kelsey, a fast winger on our team. Kelsey ran it the last few yards full of open muddy grass to score the first try of the game! We had won, and it was the best feeling ever. The taste of victory is the best taste ever, and I knew I would want to experience this again!

We all crowded around Kelsey and hugged each other. Then we shook the other team's hands to seal our win. I said good-bye to my parents and thanked them for coming. Dad said that we would discuss my future as a rugby player when I got home that night. I ran back into the school, changed at fast speeds and ran into the gym. I didn't even get a chance to look at myself because I ran past the mirrors so we could start practicing badminton. I saw a coach in the hall on the way and she said, 'Whoa, better get cleaned up. On your way to the bathroom?' I just continued on to the gym and nodded because I didn't want to keep Miles waiting.

I ran into the gym and Miles burst out laughing and went and grabbed his phone. I was like, 'What?

What's so funny?' I told him that we won! And just as I told him, he held the cell phone up like he was texting somebody, then I heard the click and realized he had taken a picture of me! I guess my whole face was covered with mud!

'Miles, you totally have to delete that picture. That's horrible! I look like a monster!'

'Ha-ha, nope, you'll never get it,' said Miles with a grin.

'Fine, then, I'll wipe mud all over you,' I replied.

I dodged for the phone as he held it up high, our bodies got tangled, and I felt a tingle as I touched his skin and wiped mud all over his face! We play fought for the phone until I finally surrendered. There was now mud all over the ground, and I realized I still had my rugby socks on that had been completely drenched in mud. Miles looked down and we both started laughing at the realization of the mess we had made. I asked if he had another pair of socks. He said yes, but they were smelly. We both ran and got paper towels to clean up before anybody witnessed the mess we had made in the gym, and I put on his socks.

Wow, boys' socks stink! Plus it didn't help that I had kid-sized feet and he had giant feet! I had to pull them up to my knees like the stylish olden day kids. Apparently that's why styles go out the back door . . . because they are hideous!

Miles and I continued the evening with our last hard-core practice. I didn't go to basketball practice that night because my coach knew I had CWOSSA in two days and said I was allowed to focus on that.

It was two days before CWOSSA so we wanted to work on everything, but not get hurt. Jonah, one of my grounder boys, came and helped us out. He is this crazy talented guy. The singles player, Brodie, also invited us out to the club to practice a few days a week to prepare. Miles and I played our men's doubles team. We were pretty evenly matched, which was shocking because usually men's doubles kill a mixed team because mixed teams have a girl.

It was a blast playing with all the boys and being the only girl left in badminton. I think my tomboyish roots came out a bit. It was also cool to get all the attention. But sometimes it sucked because they would talk 'boy talk' and I just kind of sat by myself.

I had survived my last rugby game before CWOSSA and Miles would find out about co-pres tomorrow. The stress was on. We left the gym late after an awesome practice. I headed home to talk to Papa Bear and convince him rugby was safe, and Miles was headed home to stay up and worry all night about the election. It was so odd that we had lives outside of badminton; sometimes it felt like that was my whole life. I mean, when I left the gym it was all I thought about anyway. I was starting to feel like Miles and badminton were a part of my life all the time, even if I wasn't with him or the sport.

Preparation

> *Aim for success, not perfection.*
> *Never give up your right to be wrong,*
> *because then you will lose the ability*
> *to learn new things and*
> *move forward with your life.*
>
> —David M. Burns

I woke up and felt like I hadn't slept at all. I just wanted to lay in bed forever, wrap my head up in the covers, and forget about the world. I was about to cocoon myself and just lay there when I heard Mom calling, 'Wake up, children, it's a beautiful day.' I slowly got out of bed and looked out the window. I guess what one person thinks is beautiful is ugly to another. The cold outdoors didn't look too welcoming, but I knew this day was going to begin whether I was a part of it or not. I hopped out of bed and put some clothes on. I went downstairs and had a half a bagel with some peanut butter and sliced bananas on it. My favourite! I loved breakfast;

it was by far the best meal of the day. I loved how breakfast foods were allowed to be horrible for your body but it still counted as a meal. Who invented all those cereals like Lucky Charms and Froot Loops anyway? I doubt there were any healthy ingredients in those cereals, but they tasted great!

    I was ready for school and waiting yet again for my sister to be ready. Sure, she woke up before me, but I was always ready before her. I didn't understand why she wore makeup. I thought she was gorgeous and didn't need it one bit. I think some people just rely on makeup to make them feel better, and then they get stuck and can't live without it. They start wearing makeup, and then that is what they expect when they look in the mirror. They expect the face with makeup, and when they don't see it, they load on the makeup to conform to what is expected. Anyway, I didn't mind. It meant that I would get shotgun. I have no idea why people always try and get shotgun. When I think about it, I don't actually mind sitting in the back at all. Plus it's the safest spot to be in a car accident. I just liked the satisfaction of winning the shotgun competition and beating her to it every time. Personally, I loved competition and I would take any opportunity I could to win. I started thinking about shotgun and decided that sometimes I would race to the car just to 'shotgun' backseat. I bet if you raced for the backseat you would always win. I considered this option, but my heart for competition overcame my heart to win and I raced my sister for the front seat.

    Our car pulled into the school parking lot and you could feel the excitement. Everybody knew it was Election Day. Even the smoking pit took a break from killing their lungs to come to classes so they could vote. The future of our school would be decided. Even though I wouldn't be going back to high school, it was still a huge decision and I wanted Miles to clean up. He deserved to win and win by a landslide! He had the best videos and posters and he would do the best job. He was the perfect balance between being popular and somebody who cared. It was crazy, but somehow he managed to be both. I never really noticed Miles as being somebody so cool; I always thought of him as just being there and being somebody that was in a completely different social realm than I was. Sure, we went to some of the same parties and had mutual friends, but outside of badminton we weren't really 'tight like Spandex', I guess you could say. I think because I was friends with his twin sister there was that sort of brother-like boundary that just made us all forget about him, but he was starting to become visible and I didn't really know how to react. I tried to be his sister's friend first and Miles' badminton partner second; everything else would just have to wait, maybe even forever.

The assembly to announce the winner was finally here. After a morning of telling everybody—even people I didn't recognize—to vote for Miles, I felt like I had done my job. It was so hard because I was in grade twelve and a lot of my friends were running. I tried to support them all, but I supported Miles and had my hopes for who I wanted to win with him. People understood that Miles was my badminton partner and that was why he was the only person

I publically admitted to following 100 percent, but really there was more to me wanting Miles to win then just being my badminton partner. There was more to us than just being partners, even if I hadn't realized it yet.

The announcement started with our vice principal congratulating all of the people who ran and all their hard work…blah blah blah…Then came the moment that would decide our high school's fate. All I heard was the vice principal continue: 'We would like to congratulate our 20011-2012 co-presidents Kendall Green, and MILES!!!' The audience erupted into applause and we couldn't even hear the rest of the announcement! Somehow in the midst of the cheering and jumping, Miles ended up in my arms in a huge hugging jumping celebration. Kendall and Miles hopped up on the stage for a thank-you speech. I could tell Miles had almost completely relaxed and I was hoping that would be good for badminton.

After the rest of the day of celebration, we had a quick badminton practice before CWOSSA. Miles and I just played for an hour and I felt like he didn't really care. I understood that he had to relax after such stress had just been relieved, but maybe after something so important, badminton wouldn't matter to him anymore. I stayed a little after Miles left and Brodie, the singles player, helped me with my serve.

Brodie was one of the top athletes at our school. He was one of those guys that you would hear coming before they actually passed you in the halls. He carried a sense of awe with him. Every guy looked up to him and he was a man's man. I talked to Brodie a bit, but I always felt like he should be too cool for me, especially when he hung out with 'the boys' or the hockey all-stars. Brodie was actually a really nice guy, and he spent a long time coaching me, it's just that he belonged on a different social scale than me. He was the kind of guy that lived one day at a time and only worried about the present. Brodie lived for sports and dominated them, but he didn't go to class and I could tell he was getting worried about his future. I was really bonding with Brodie that night, and I asked him what he would do after high school. He just laughed and said that his life would be over after high school, that he couldn't make it in the real world and he would be a bum for the rest of his life. That's why badminton, his final sport, would be very important. We cleaned up the nets and walked out of the gym.

    I left with a sense that Brodie could change the world if only somebody believed in him. I wished that I could provide him with the support and coaching he had given me. I wished I could help him with his future just like he helped me with my unstoppable serve. I left with the passion to win tomorrow and nerves that could have killed me.

Competition

*Strength does not come from physical capacity;
it comes from an indomitable will.*

—Gandhi

When you wake up on important days of your life there is a lingering sense of curiosity in the air. The air is so thick and still that you know something is different. On every important day so far in my life I have been startled awake extremely early. Not woken up by the dog or loud neighbors, just by emotion. You wake up at ridiculous hours and have no idea why. You know you should fall back asleep because sleep is essential for success, but you can't. No matter how hard you try to fall back asleep, your body just won't let you. The worst part is, the harder you try to fall asleep, the further away you get from it actually happening. Well, this is what happened to me.

I rolled over in my bed thinking that it was time to get ready for CWOSSA, getting ready to pack my gym bag, getting ready to face fate. Then I looked at the clock . . . 5:00 a.m. was what I saw, those beautiful green lights of the clock radio just glowing at me, taunting me. *This is ridiculous,* I thought. I thought that time was supposed to be constant, but those minutes and seconds passed by more slowly than when you're waiting to go into the dentist's office and all the magazines in the waiting room are taken. Those seconds felt like hours, and the more I thought about time and how slow it was passing, the longer it took for them to pass.

Finally, after many daydreams, 7:00 a.m. rolled around, and I hopped out of bed and got dressed. I grabbed my gym bag and went down to eat breakfast. I let the dog out to pee and looked outside at the hazy morning dew. It seemed to be a nice day, although a little on the chilly side. I made my half a bagel with peanut butter and bananas and ate my favorite breakfast. Mom came down and asked if I had had anything to drink. I always forget to drink, it's just such a hassle and it's always so cold on my throat. I said no and she poured me some orange juice. I drank two sips, trying to make it seem like I had gulped down the whole glass.

I was just about to go to the car as she asked if I had packed a lunch. Oh no, I had forgotten. Mom just smiled, as she had done it for me. She handed me my lunch bag with a sandwich, some carrots, granola bars, grapes and an apple. Then she handed me a Banana Strawberry Smoothie bottle. It looked similar to a Gatorade container but a bit bigger. I told her that I was okay and would just drink water, but she said I needed something to keep my energy levels up. Plus, she knew I wasn't kidding anybody when I said I would drink water. I took the smoothie container and shoved my food in my bag. I grabbed my shoes and went to the front door to wait for Miles and Brodie to pick me up. I was just looking out the window as they pulled into my driveway. I ran to the car, and the day began.

We got to the crowded gym and sat in the same place in the stands that Billa-Aid always sits. Jonah and the rest of the guys were already there, as were our coaches. Curly was a young coach and I loved her as a person, but she stayed in the shadows to learn from the head coach who had been around longer. I related very well to Curly because she was younger and we shared lots of the same interests. The boys double team and our boys single players all belonged to a badminton club outside of school, so they provided lots of individual coaching and advice.

The first game Miles and I played went by quickly. The other team hardly got any points at all. It was like we were playing against elementary school children. Then we had to wait for two hours until our next game. We were stuck sitting in the stands watching other games and attempting homework that we both knew would never get accomplished. Tournaments were so much fun; you got to hang out and escape from the realities of the real world. You could meet new people and forget all about the deadlines and decisions you had breathing down your neck. We scouted out the competition and built up some nerves for our next game.

Our next few games were very tough, but Miles and I were unstoppable. Every point and hit came so effortlessly, we were like the same person in two bodies. Miles and I covered the whole court; there wasn't anywhere they could hit that we couldn't reach. My serve was working and Miles smashed like a monster. Teams were scared of us, and we played to other teams' weaknesses.

Even if we were expected to win, I felt the tightness in my stomach as we waited at the sidelines for the game before ours to end. I hated being the expected champion, I much rather liked being the underdog and having to prove your success. Before each game we played, we had to go and sit down beside the court when our team was on deck. Miles and I would go down courtside and stretch and listen to music and try to distract ourselves and not psych ourselves out. I always felt nervous, but the games that I was most scared to play turned out to be the best. I think getting nervous or scared actually showed that I cared a lot and helped me warm up because my heart rate was accelerating on nerves alone.

Miles and I were called on to warm up as the game before us finished. We always warmed up with our sweatshirts on. It was true intimidation. Miles would listen to music while he warmed up, but I could never keep the iPod headphones in my ears so I would just warm up without music. Sometimes I would have a song stuck in my head and sing along or make up my own song, but most of the time I was just scouting the other team as we warmed up. Miles and I were always very polite to the other team; we didn't want to make enemies—our parents had raised us well. So far it seemed to be in our favor. Even if we beat a team earlier, they were here cheering for us now. It was pretty cool having all these fans.

The games were getting tougher and tougher and there were fewer and fewer schools represented at the gym as team after team was eliminated. Miles went to look at the schedule to see who we would play next. Curly came and gave me her scouting report. She said that we would have to play a brother-sister team who were ranked first nationally. They had won nationals last year and it would be the older sister's last opportunity to play badminton in high school. Their whole family was there cheering them on, and I mean cousins, aunts, and uncles. It was a big deal in their family, and their dad videotaped every game to send to scouts for scholarship opportunities. I'm pretty sure the dad had called some scouts to come watch. The stakes were high, and we were the underdogs.

Miles came back and his face showed that he had heard about the unstoppable siblings. He also brought back news saying that Northview had lost to this sibling team and was now on the losing side of the bracket. We would play this sibling team for the finals or semis, depending on wins and losses. We didn't play for another four games, and I didn't know if I would make it that long. I called my parents and told them the news. They said they would be on their way to watch. Curly built me up, saying that we could do it, that I was the best girl she had ever seen, and that Miles had my back. She said we just needed confidence and we could do anything.

Brodie had lost his second game and now he was sure that he would not be moving on. It was the end of Brodie's athletic career at Billa-Aid. He would be thrown into the real world after this summer—well, at least the real world of post-secondary education. Billa-Aid's morale was low as our mixed team was called to double deck. Miles and I just looked at each other. I told him I needed to go for a quick walk. I went out in the hall and had an apple as I walked around and out to the fresh air. I was so scared; I didn't want my badminton career to come to an end just like Brodie's. I walked back into the gym and sat beside Miles.

Miles just looked at me and said, "This is our time; we can do it. Let's go to OFSAA, Riley!" OFSAA was the big leagues; it meant Ontario Federation of School Athletic Associations. Miles had passion and fury in his eyes. He cared about this more than the election the previous days, maybe even more than anything in his life before. This was our chance to prove we were the best at something, to prove that we were heroes. To prove that, despite the fact that we didn't belong to private clubs or have years and years of training, we could be just as good—if not better than—everybody else. Miles and I walked down to the courts once the game before us had reached third set. We never go down too early so that we don't get cramped from sitting too long. I had my twenty-dollar Canadian tire racket in hand and goggles on my forehead, and we were ready to face our destiny.

The game before ours went very long and it was super close. I was glad we weren't sitting there before that set like the brother-sister team. We both leaned against the wall and stretched as the final points were played out. Then the birdie dropped and the game was over, captains went to sign the sheet, and Miles and I took over the court. I went under the net to the far side and we put our goggles on and started clearing the birdie in high powerful shots, just whacking that thing as hard as we could to get our nerves out. Then we practiced smashes and drops and serves, and before we knew it, our warm up was over and it was game time.

There were fewer games going on at once because people had been eliminated. They announced our game on the big speakers. The crowd up in the stands formed and even some coaches came to floor level and crowded our court. The sibling team's dad had the camera rolling, and the birdie toss determined who had first serve. I threw the birdie up and it landed pointing at the siblings. Miles and I handed the birdie over because they wanted serve, and then we met in our court and gave each other a team handshake to begin the game. It was a motivation you-can-do-it-let's-cream-these-guys kind of handshake.

The older sister served the birdie first. She served to me, and I returned her high lob serve with an alley smash. It was a good start. Most people serve long to girls because they can't smash very well and have a hard time getting back quickly enough. This was my specialty because of my years of volleyball training, plus Brodie had worked on it with me. Now it was my turn to see if my serve would hold up in a high stakes game.

I walked up to the serving 'T'. Miles gave me a high five, and then I held the birdie and racket below my waist and tried out my new serve. I held my breath and froze as it crossed the net; the sister tried to lunge for it, but it was out of her reach! I had aced one of the best badminton players in Canada! I turned to Miles, and he looked just as shocked as I felt! He gave me a huge hug and was like, 'Wow, Riley that was amazing! We're off to a good start; we just have to remember to keep reacting and stay focused.'

It was time to face the brother. I served him my same new serve, but my racket just clipped my finger and I knew we would be in trouble. The brother whacked the birdie hard and to the back left of the court. Miles retaliated with a huge backhand smash! It was incredible. Miles and I were on, and we weren't going to let anything happen to this match. The brother was like, 'Can we get a drink?' Miles and I just looked at each other as if to say, 'Sure, why not?' We didn't really know all these rules. We usually just played through the sets and took breaks and coaching advice in between sets. The brother was very whiney and quite annoying. He would make crazy remarks after each point and huff and puff. After each point we had won so far, the brother and sister would go into the middle of the court, and she would just hold his shoulders as he would complain and place blame.

I continued serving stealthily, even after their strange water break. Although we lost the serve a few times, we came back with determination. We won our first set 21-6, and we could tell that they were agitated. It wasn't that they were a bad team; Miles and I just played to the end of every bird. We didn't let anything touch the ground unless we full out dove and still came short. It was one of the most intense games I had ever been a part of. Even though it was 'only badminton', it felt like it was the Olympics. The crowd was into it and screaming after every point, and the siblings' parents could be heard over everybody. Normally badminton was a quiet 'gentleman's' game, if you will, but today after every point the crowd would erupt in cheering. The skill and talent that was represented here in this final match was incredible. I'm pretty sure even if the siblings lost, the dad would send in the tape to the scouts because it was so good that even the loser looked phenomenal.

After our first set, our coaches came down and so did Jonah and his partner. They said to keep doing what we were doing and not let the little boy get into our heads. We had to play strong and utilize the girl's backhand weakness. The boy had amazing lateral movement, so we were supposed to try some cross-drop shots, but only if we were sure the girl couldn't cut anything off and smash it back in our faces. We were feeling pretty pumped, and I couldn't see past anything but the first serve.

We walked back on the court and the other team was still talking. Miles and I just waited and talked in the middle of the court. When it finally became ridiculous that they were still talking, we asked them if we could begin. The boy looked at us, and said with some hand motions, 'We can take as long as we want.' Miles and I, shocked at the rude response, just stood at the server line and waited. They finally came to the court after the crowd booed at the response and the convener asked if they could begin. We could tell that temperatures were rising and attitudes wouldn't be as polite.

They served to start off the game. Miles quickly sent a long clear to the back left corner and the brother sent a drop shot cross-court. I was there and cut it off, which means I smashed it right down so nobody even had a chance to get it. After we had won that point, we high-fived and got ready to serve. It was strange; they just replayed the point and practiced some footwork. We were flabbergasted, and asked, 'Um, can you please continue with the game?' So we proceeded on. This game was a lot closer than the last game; it was point for point. We were down by one and Miles was getting rattled. Then they clear served it to Miles and he smashed it into the net. This would not be good for our team.

We were down by two and coming to the end of the game. They served to me short, and I tried to send a drop shot return straight across the net, but I sent it too short. It hit the top of the net and trickled back on our side. I whacked my racket into the back of my thigh. Whenever I missed a shot I would hit the back of my leg as instant reaction. I sometimes got bruises on the back of my leg. Miles asked if he could have a drink as he walked over to his red Gatorade. The brother was like, 'Um, excuse me, you cannot have a drink unless we approve it, and we don't approve that this is a good time for a drink!' Miles had the Gatorade bottle close to his lips, so he looked up in the stands at the Northview coach, who shouted, 'Drink it, Miles, drink it! That isn't the rule; you're allowed to drink!' Miles brought the Gatorade bottle the rest of his way to his lips and he took two long sips!

The brother started freaking out. 'But that's not fair, that isn't the rules, you should be disqualified!' The sister just looked at her brother and agreed with some angry hand-flailing actions. I loved Miles for taking that sip; we had finally stood up for ourselves against this team with all their little rules and cheap calls. This team was getting on my nerves. At first I was scared for what Miles was going to do. I had lived my life making friends and following the rules, making people happy, but for once Miles had done what he wanted, and it felt good to be on his team supporting him. Then he walked back to the court and said "all ready" in the brother's high-pitched voice with some hand actions. The crowd erupted in laughter and even the convener was smiling. Apparently the convener hadn't heard of that rule either, and he was glad that Miles had followed his urge to have a drink.

After the Gatorade incident the game took a spin and we got three aces in a row. It was game point, and you could cut the tension with a knife. The gym was silent as Miles served short to the boy; he returned it with a high lob to the middle of the court. I looked back, which I have never done before in my badminton career, and I saw Miles approach the high mid-court birdie. He had a sparkle in his eyes, and I knew he was going to cream this bad boy! He jumped up and spiked it straight down the left alley, and the brother and sister both dove to their death. They both came short and ran into each other. They looked up to see if their fate was real. The crowd stood in applause and cheering, and the whole gym was surrounding our court!

The parents of the brother and sister were bawling their eyes out, and the dad turned off the video camera and looked down in shame. The brother and sister were both still on the ground, tangled in a mess of their bodies and emotions. They just started crying as they realized they had been beaten. They had been beaten by nobodies, people they had never even heard of before. The team that beat them didn't even have rackets from a pro shop or proper training.

Miles and I looked at each other and then looked around and soaked up all the appreciation and cheering. After all, they were cheering for us! It was an incredible moment, and after we looked around I ran to Miles and jumped into his arms. He swung me around in a huge hug, and I never wanted him to let me go! He kissed me on the forehead as we just stood there and hugged. The moment was unforgettable. We had just beaten the national champions, and we would be going to provincials to see if we could beat the teams they had conquered the year before. We just stood in the embrace for minutes in pure joy. Then we walked to the net holding hands, where we eventually let go to shake the other team's hands. I told the sister that she was incredibly good and that her short game was the best I had ever seen. Miles apologized for taking a drink, and they just looked at each other and walked off the court in defeat. They went and complained to their high status coach and parents.

The brother-sister team would still have another game to see if they would be the second team moving on. If the brother and sister team won, they would be the second team and we would be in first; if they lost, we would have to play another team to defend our title. We felt like we had won everything there was in the world to win and walked up to the stands with huge smiles on our face. It was like we had big clown grins plastered on our faces, and they couldn't come off. I walked into our section and everybody just started clapping and cheering. I tried not to smile, but I couldn't help but show all my teeth. I turned to Miles and he had the same goofy grin plastered on his face still. I figured I wouldn't try to hide this smile and just embraced it!

Everybody gave us huge hugs and compliments, telling us it was the best game they had ever seen. Then Curly came over and told us that, no matter what, we would be given an OFSAA bid! We were going to provincials! This was huge. We would get to go and compete for the best in Ontario and, hopefully, all of Canada! But Curly had more to say. She said that the brother-sister team would have to play Northview, and if they lost, we would play Northview for the first place bid, but if they won, we wouldn't have to play another game.

I still couldn't wipe my goofy smile off my face, and Miles seemed to have the same problem. Miles came up from behind me and gave me a huge hug. I could get used to this living in bliss and happiness all the time! I could get used to being in Miles' arms.

I personally wanted the Northview team to come with us to the provincial tournament, OFSAA, because I would have to room with whichever girl went, and they were way nicer then the brother-sister team. Plus if the brother-sister team came with us to provincials, they would probably have a room together and Miles and I would be put with random people.

We went down on floor level to cheer our men's doubles team on. They didn't have any real competition here at this tournament. They were in the finals against a team they had played a thousand times over the years. They had only beaten them twice. I got the feeling that they were happy as long as they got to provincials. They were goofing off and chirping each other throughout the game. They ended up losing in three games, but they were completely happy with that. I think they wanted to be the underdog at provincials.

Billa-Aid High School had four players going to OFSAA. This was more than they had ever had before. We would be a highly represented school at the all—Ontario competition! Usually only one or two players (if any) got to go to OFSAA. Our school went to quad 'A' provincials; that meant it was the best of the best! Miles and I just had to see if we were going as a first seed or if we would have another game. We went to cheer on the Northview team.

Northview won the first set, but the brother-sister team won the second. The third game was close, and we were cheering for Northview even though we were standing beside the parents of the brother and sister. The brother-sister team went on a five-point run, and we could tell Northview was in trouble. Northview ended up being unable to recover, and the brother-sister team won with a six-point lead. The parents started cheering like animals, but the majority of the crowd had been cheering for Northview. The Northview boy and girl just shook hands and then they talked to their coach. A few tears trickled down their faces.

The male Northview player had come back a fifth year just to go to OFSAA; he had been through cancer a few years before and he had been clear for two years now. This was his one chance to get back into sports and prove he was still talented. He had practiced every day at the club on top of the school training. I felt bad that they wouldn't be coming with us. Despite the fact that we had an ongoing rivalry, they were polite and we became frienimies (friendly enemies). We were even Facebook friends. Miles and I went up and congratulated both teams, and then we stayed to talk to Northview. We told them that we had wished it was their team with us instead. The brother-sister coach stole the male Northview player and told him how awesome his game was. This was just harder for him and made the loss even harder to swallow.

The convener called us up to the podium for our medals because we were officially number one. It was now a bittersweet win; knowing we were number one was awesome but knowing that the brother and sister team was number two was tough. We got our medals and Miles gave me a massive hug sealing our official win. The crowd was all in favour of our win and everybody was cheering. It was such a cool feeling to be the winners and the favourites; it made it more special since we came in as underdogs.

We went up to our area in the stands afterwards, and my parents asked if we wanted to go eat. They thought we must have been starving. I was like, 'What? Why? What time is it?' Mom said that it was 9:00 p.m., and I could hardly believe it! I had no idea where the day went.

I went out for dinner with my parents and then hit the homework; after all, it was back to reality tomorrow and I would have to face school and the real world!

Aftermath

*'Who are you?' said the caterpillar.
'I hardly know, sir.
Just at present—
at least I know who I was
when I got up this morning,
but I think I've changed
several times since then.'*

—*Alice in Wonderland,* by Lewis Carroll

The next day wasn't quite back to reality just yet. The whole school knew about our amazing win, and the few people that didn't know coming into school heard about it after the announcements. There was a huge article about Billa-Aid High School's amazing badminton players. We were like celebrities—everybody congratulated us and provided special treatment for us.

Brodie and I had the same English class. Our English teacher asked for our essays that were due. I had gone home and worked on mine, but Brodie didn't have his finished. Our English teacher just looked at both of us and said, 'Oh, if you two need extra time, take it; you guys don't need to hand it in today. You've had a stressful little while.' It took me a minute to get what he was saying. He said we didn't need to hand it in today! What!?!? I had never been treated with such favouritism. I handed mine in anyway because I just wanted it to be done, but it was cool to be recognized.

It made me wonder what would have happened if we hadn't won and hadn't been recognized in the paper. Would we have just been forgotten and blended in with the faceless mass and the rest of the students? It is crazy how certain accomplishments are meaningful and others go unnoticed. I wondered who made that decision and why there were amazing kids out there going unnoticed and unrecognized.

I was walking to the gym after school to get changed for rugby practice when I saw the bulletin board with the picture of me and Miles on it. They had already put up a picture of us with our medals. Wow! The school was so proud of us, and it was so strange. Even my rugby coach knew about our win, and Coach never paid any attention to anything other than rugby! The world had been turned upside down and I no longer knew my role. People who I hardly talked to were giving me high fives and hugs in the halls. I was not a very touchy-feely person and I usually liked my personal bubble and my own space. It was so strange to adapt to all the attention. I continued on into the gym and talked to Curly and our other coaches. They said we would get today off because we needed to rest and recuperate. Then we would have three practices before OFSAA.

I would have three rugby practices as well and no games because we got a bye that week. My life was working out perfectly. Although I would have to miss one rugby game due to provincials, I was hoping it wouldn't be our last, but we were facing a team that goes to Ireland every year and usually wins the Irish tournament. We didn't really stand a chance. So I continued to go to practices and try to support the team as best as I could. Our rugby team would not only be missing me but most of our fifth year and fourth year players because they would be going on a camping trip.

We had to figure out rooming for OFSAA. I had hoped Curly would come and be able to room with me. She was twenty-six and acted just like a friend; if I didn't room with her, I would have to room with a complete stranger. I could see myself being Curly's friend outside of school and since she was a coach and never my teacher our friendship was deeper. The other three boys were allowed to room together (our boys doubles team and Miles).

The next three days were a blur. I concentrated on completing the schoolwork that I would miss, getting people to cover my work shifts, and going to all the practices. Practices were easy and we didn't switch anything; we just tried to perfect our shots and work on patience. Before I knew it, it was the day before OFSAA.

Miles and I went to school and grabbed our last-minute assignments. School was coming to an end and most of our summatives (final projects worth a bunch of marks) were due. I had done most of mine the previous week to get them out of the way, but they wouldn't be due until after OFSAA. I went to all of my classes and all of the teachers wished us good luck. It was like the whole school was on board and going to OFSAA along with us.

I was supposed to take it easy at rugby practice or just watch. I went and just did some lineouts and helped Coach more than anything. Everybody was scared I would get hurt and I wasn't allowed to ruin our school's chances of doing well at OFSAA. I came back from rugby practice all in one piece, and then we had a meeting instead of a practice filled with drills and games for badminton.

Curly gave us a packing list and told us that we had to be at the school at 7:00 a.m. the next morning so that we could get on the road and arrive at OFSAA in good time. OFSAA was being held in Sudbury, Ontario, which is about a six-hour car ride from Billa-Aid High School. Our other head coach said that the schedule would be a 'play it by ear' win-lose situation so we wouldn't really know until we got there. She said to go home and get lots of rest because tomorrow would be the start of some of the most important days of our lives. Little did I know that my important moments would be starting in just a few hours.

Less Than A Blink

*The real test of character is in surprise.
It is unforeseen crisis,
the sudden calamity,
the unexpected shock,
when the man is off guard,
which shows truly what he is.*

—Archibald Macmechan

I got home from school ridiculously early because I had no athletics after school, just that quick badminton meeting. It felt odd. Today was the day that was going to change the course of my grade twelve year in ways nobody expected. I was excited all day because of OFSAA, so when I got home I decided to pack first and then conquer homework.

    I put on my badminton goggles to try them out and grabbed my jersey and shorts to put in my bag. I took the goggles off and threw them in my bag. Then I packed all the jerseys I had collected from other badminton players. I collected other jerseys so I could have more than one to wear throughout the OFSAA competition so I wouldn't be stinky.

I went to go grab my gym bag from the closet. When I opened it up I saw that old smoothie bottle my Mom had given me for my last tournament just sitting unopened in my bag. I decided I should probably clean out my bag before I packed, so I decided to empty the smoothie bottle and throw it away. As soon as I grabbed the bottle and positioned it upright and vertical as I walked across the hall to the bathroom, the bottle exploded, collapsing my OFSAA dreams with it.

As banana strawberry smoothie flew in the air, eventually landing to stain the carpet, the lid flew off the bottle and nailed me in the eye! I did not even have time to blink, so my eye was open when the lid hit me. It was so powerful I fell down with the force, getting whiplash. Little did I know the whiplash was the least of my worries. The lid bounced off the wall after it hit and slashed my eye and then landed six feet away by my brother's room. It was so powerful that when it hit the wall it left a dent behind. The smoothie bottle explosion could be the new weapon of mass destruction that they were looking for; it was ridiculously powerful.

As the explosion happened, my family reacted in their own individual ways. My brother dropped the phone in mid-conversation with his buddy (they were planning tennis for the next day). He came out of his room and asked if I was okay. Brianne, my younger, sister looked out of her room while the smoothie was exploding and witnessed some of it. She then saw my parents coming, yelled no particular words at all, and then slammed the door and hid in her room. She was in complete shock and just sat there shaking, trying to shut out the image she had just witnessed. Mom said some words that I have never ever heard her say before that were definitely not G-rated and rushed to my side. As she took the spot beside me, my brother left and started using the computer to Google eye traumas. Dad came booming up the stairs yelling 'WHAT'S WRONG?!? Is THAT blood?!' wrongly accusing the smoothie spill of being blood. Mom told me to try and open my eye. So I did, and she screamed and ran to the phone.

My reaction when I was hit by the lid was to fall down because of force. My head actually whipped back and smacked the wall, and then I fell down and laughed for a few seconds of initial shock. I continued to say I was fine to my assisting brother, who knew I wasn't and wouldn't be 'fine' for a while. Then I just sat there feeling nothing—and I mean nothing. I couldn't feel my body. I could not feel any emotion. It was like chaos had erupted around me and I was frozen, not a part of any of it. Except I was the center of attention; I was the accident.

As I opened my eye for Mom, I realized I could not see anything. I was blind in my right eye. I was somewhat calm because I knew that everything would be all right. The sound in the world slowly came back, but it felt like nobody was there because I felt so calm and at ease. I knew that everything would work out, so I shouldn't worry. I figured

OFSAA would still be in the next day's game plan. But I was completely wrong.

Apparently, when I opened my eye, all Mom saw was blood—no white and brown like my normal blink would have shown.

Mom called Nathan Key, my friend's father and an optometrist, to see if he could help. First she called my aunt to try and get a hold of my uncle who is an optometrist. He was in meetings and unavailable. This was an emergency and my family could sense it. Dad started cleaning up the smoothie to keep himself busy, my sister Brianne stayed in hiding, and Carter was watching eye surgeries on YouTube. As Mom called Nathan and described my vampire eye to him, he told us to keep me upright; he would drive by our house and lead the way to his office. He was on his way home from work when we reached him on his cell. He hadn't even eaten dinner yet, but he just kept driving and led us to his office, realizing the seriousness of the situation.

Dad was a professor and had been about to leave for a class at Laurier. He made sure we left all right and kept his phone on to continue on the shortest business lecture ever. His class started at 7 p.m. and ended only a few minutes after. The explosion had gone off at 6:27 p.m. Once Mom got everything sorted out with Nathan and was sure that he was on his way to our house, she got me settled in the car. She had to lead me to the car because both my eyes naturally went shut. Once I was in the car, I was sitting there looking uncomfortable. Mom gave me her sunglasses and put the pedal to the metal. My brother and sister were left to finish their homework and clean up the mess that I had left behind, but they could not clean up the changed perspective or the silent coat of fear in the air.

Rubble

*The fact is
that to do anything in the world worth doing,
we must not stand back
shivering and thinking of the cold and danger,
but jump in and scramble through
as well as we can.*

—Robert Crashing

Mom and I reached Nathan's office in record time. The whole way there I prayed Mom would drive safely and keep herself safe. As we zoomed out of my driveway, I said, 'Mom, please just drive safe . . . we don't need to endanger ourselves right now. That won't help anything.' I don't know whether it was because my eyes were closed or whether Mom's protective bear instinct kicked in, but I could have sworn we were in NASCAR's Daytona 500.

I now realize what the protective bear instinct is. It's what kicks in when, no matter who stands in your way, if your child is hurt, you're going to protect them at any cost. Mom was driving like an angry grizzly bear to protect me and get me to safety faster. I feel sorry for all the cars on those roads that night because anything in her way didn't stand a chance.

Nathan Key's office was a very nice house-like building. Mom described this to me because the light seemed to hurt my eyes too much. Even when I had her sunglasses on and my eyes closed, I felt irritated. My body was still in shock so irritation and discomfort were the closest feelings I had to true emotion. It was dinnertime for the rest of the city, but for me food and a nice meal was the last thing on my mind.

Having my eyes closed and not being able to see would shortly become my reality, and Mom hadn't even begun her sacrifices by giving me her sunglasses. The office was quiet and only one secretary remained. We went right into Nathan's office. As he left briefly, Mom made some gagging sounds and I thought she was going to be sick to her stomach. She may have already realized the seriousness of the situation.

This was the first eye examination chair I sat in, but it was definitely not the last. Nathan came back into the room with many drops. He first looked in my eye through a slit lamp. He tried to hide the shock, but as air escaped his lips, I knew he didn't like what he saw. He had to hold my eyelid open because I couldn't seem to open it by myself. He immediately put a cornea bandage contact lens on to hold the eye together. The thought that I needed something to hold my eye together and in place sends chills down my spine. Dr. Key explained that my cornea was lacerated, sliced in half. He also said my eye appeared red because the blood cavity behind the lens of the eye had filled with blood from the force of the impact. In medical terms, a blood-red eye is referred to as a hyphema. The blood was contained in my eye, but it could take months and months to reabsorb this blood back into my body. I guessed I would look like a vampire for a while.

Dr. Key left the room and talked to the only person left in the office. It was eerily quiet and we could hear him speaking through the walls and closed door. He spoke in a rushed quiet tone and the secretary quickly made a phone call after the brief conversation. He came back into our eye examining room and saw Mom's ghostly face.

He was the bearer of bad news. He said he just called the hospital's ophthalmology surgeon and made an appointment for first thing in the morning. Nothing could be done tonight. Dr. Key said I would have to remain upright with my head above my heart for the rest of the night. He put multiple pressure and freezing drops into my eye to try to give me some stability for a few hours. He gave me more drops to dilate the pupil. This was just the beginning of eye drops in my life; I would soon have a broad collection. I did not understand what his words and these actions meant for my life. I was in robot mode and could not form opinions or thoughts. My body moved from home to the office but somewhere along the way my smiley athlete identity was lost.

Shattered?

> *Anybody can give up,*
> *it's the easiest thing in the world to do;*
> *but to hold on when everyone else*
> *would understand if you fell apart,*
> *that's true strength.*

We drove home around 9:30 p.m. with a new perspective and fear instilled in us. The moment I first felt the pain and reality of the situation was in Dr. Key's chair. He was explaining the medical mumbo jumbo and I asked him one question... I asked the only question that seemed to matter. I asked, 'Can I still go to OFSAA, can I go to provincials?' The look on his face and the silence told it all. At this point the freezing drops allowed me to open my good eye, but I wished it was still stuck shut so I didn't have to witness the look of absolute hopelessness. Even squinting through one eye, I could see that he was devastated, and no matter how hard he tried to hide his disappointment, the pain shined through. He responded, 'Riley, we'll see, but I don't think OFSSA is even an option . . .' as he said this I stopped holding my breath and started crying.

I could not contain the tears that streamed down my face, or stop my uncontrollable shaking. I couldn't let Miles, my badminton partner, down. This was the highlight of our high school careers, and I had just destroyed it. I ruined Miles' most exciting moment. How could I tell him? I was happy I was blind—well, at least in one eye—so I didn't have to see his face fall when I told him the news. But Miles wasn't what Dr. Keys was worried about. He wasn't finished telling us the bad news.

He continued as I held my tears and sadness in. I was just silently shaking. My eye was in unbearable pain. I had never experienced such pain before, but it seemed secondary to Miles's ruined happiness. Dr. Key said, 'Riley, what we need to worry about right now is your eye; we need to do everything in our power to make you see again.'

As he said this, Mom gasped; the thought of having me blind in one eye was too much for her to hold in. Dr. Key said he would drop by later that night to check my pressure and make sure I was stable. He was worried I would crash, and he knew the best option would be getting me to the surgeon the next morning when some of the blood had drained and I was more stable.

Once we returned home, Carter and Brianne came to meet us. Dad was on his way home from his lecture. I got out of the car and needed assistance into the house. I don't really like getting help from other people very much. I like being strong and independent, but this would be the last time in a long time that I would be able to consider myself strong. I was so weak, and I was unusually tired already.

I'm used to being strong and athletic; this experience would change my whole lifestyle. Mom led me to the big blue leather chair in our family room, usually reserved for Dad, and I slouched onto the seat, feeling dizzy. Pillows were already propped behind my head. I would have given anything to lie down sideways and just sleep. I just wanted to curl up in the comfortable fetal position and travel back a few hours. Why couldn't I be better, how could I be so stupid and not protect myself? I was wearing my badminton goggles two minutes before I grabbed my gym bag . . . if only it had happened when I was wearing them. All these doubts crossed my mind about what I could have done differently.

Then I thought this might not be real. Maybe it wasn't actually happening. After all, I didn't feel anything. *Shock* is a word that literally means you're frozen. It's like watching your body and life, while you feel hopeless and incapable of anything. It's like having a recurring nightmare when you can't do anything to prevent it or make it better. But the worst part isn't that you're incapable of changing the nightmare you're living, it's that you will never wake up from it.

Hope Exists

*The last of the human freedoms
is to choose one's attitude
in any given set of circumstances*

—Viktor E. Frankl

I got to the big chair and said, 'I need to tell Miles.' I just kept repeating myself like a broken record. Mom had called Miles' mom and asked her to bring Miles over after his shift at Apples & Oranges, our local supermarket. I asked Mom if I could just wait until the next day to tell Miles because I would be all better. Something about the situation just made me realize that I would be better. I knew that no matter what, God had a plan, and that comforted me. OFSAA had been my dream ever since I had heard the word in grade nine. We actually had a very good chance to do well. Miles and I were pros, we were good, and there was no denying it. I actually felt natural and confident in badminton. Well, I guess we *had* a good chance, until I destroyed it.

Mom threw out the bottle immediately, but she kept the warped lid. I did not know about any of this in my isolated condition. I was just happy I didn't have to go up to my room again. I was terrified to go anywhere near the accident zone. I still had hope that I would be going to OFSAA: I was going, and nobody could stop me.

My uncle came over to see my eye. He had been in a meeting all day discussing trauma and serious eye injuries. I thought it was pretty ironic how the timing had placed him in a real live trauma situation after he had talked about it all day. He looked in my eye, and I still wasn't used to the shock and disgust that instantly shot to his face. He looked at my eye further, trying to be positive and realistic at the same time. He said it wasn't just bad, it was brutal, but doctors had come a long way and there is no telling what they could fix.

I didn't even care about my eye; all I cared about was OFSAA and Miles. He was the best partner I had ever had, funny when I needed to relax but serious and competitive at other times. We had amazing chemistry on the court and could always sense where the other was on the court. We didn't even need to talk, to understand one another—we had such a strong bond. He had my back on the court and I relied and counted on him. I hope he felt at least half as confident in me. He was my badminton hero, and I never wanted anybody else. I wouldn't trade Miles as my partner for the number one Asian player in the world (everybody knew the Asians were the best at badminton). Now I had to crush this bond and break his dreams. I thought I was going to play, and didn't want to crush Miles if I didn't have to.

My uncle put more drops in my eye because the pressure and pain were just getting stronger and stronger, to the point that the pressure was so high it was scary and I was no longer stable. Miles and his mom came over; Miles was still in his polo T-shirt and work pant uniform, panic written all over his face. They came inside; I had my eyes closed, but I could sense their presence as they walked into the family room.

My uncle introduced himself and quickly left to a different room. Miles asked, 'What happened? Are you okay?'—millions of questions shooting out of his mouth with hardly any room in between to breathe. I tried to squeeze open my good eye, and I saw Miles, who looked as though he had just seen his favourite dog die in front of his very eyes. He also looked as though he was about to be sick to his stomach.

I told him what happened in a factual way. That lasted until I said the word smoothie, and then I started to cry, tears streaming down my face as I just apologized over and over again. I couldn't even feel the added pain these tears were causing. All I could feel was me chopping Miles down. He came over to my blue La-Z-Boy and held me and supported me without saying a word. Miles was there for me no matter what.

Our mothers were sitting in the kitchen, giving us enough distance so we felt like we were alone, and so Mom could tell Miles' mom what happened without me hearing, all the while staying close enough to see what was happening. I couldn't think of anything except letting Miles down. After I stopped sobbing, I just sat there in Miles' arms until our mothers re-entered the living room.

I used to be so strong that I hated it when Mom would talk or answer for me. This was the one time I don't know what I would have done without her. Mom looked at me but I couldn't speak; it was like I had been engulfed in a tornado, unable to escape or catch my breath. It was a tornado of sadness and truth, and I didn't want to let it escape my body and take over these people I cared about. So I just sat there with silent streams of truth flowing out of my eyes as I shook in sorrow.

Mom took this cue and started talking for me. She held me up in many ways, and this is just the start of how she kept me strong when I was weak. She explained, 'Riley's eye was cut in half by the lid of the smoothie bottle. We don't know much except that it's serious, there is a very limited chance she'll be going with you to OFSAA.' As soon as she said the word OFSAA, I let out a whimper, but I held that tornado in.

Miles interjected, saying, 'Riley, don't you worry about OFSAA, I just want you to be better! You were the best partner I could have wished for, and with or without OFSAA, I am very happy and proud I got to play with you! No regrets, and you better not worry about me!'

I couldn't help but let out some vocal tears, crying, 'I'm so sorry, I'm so, so sorry,' repeatedly through the tears. Before this instance, I could count the number of times I had cried on my hand.

I was a tough girl, one who didn't cry no matter how much pain I was in. Something was different about this situation, though, and I could no longer be the strong girl I used to be.

Miles' mom stepped in and said, 'Riley, all we want is for you to get better!' She then asked Mom if I would ever be able to see again. Mom looked down at her feet and responded, 'We don't know; she is seeing the surgeon first thing tomorrow and I'll let you know as soon as we hear any more!'

At this point I had quieted down my tears a bit and my uncle, brother, and sister had returned. My uncle talked with Miles about other simple, mindless things like the weather or if he liked working at Apples & Oranges. I could tell that Miles was distraught, but he was trying hard to cover it. Miles' face was filled with sadness. I'm pretty sure it wasn't for the loss of OFSAA, but for the pain I was going through.

Dad came home and threw his briefcase on the washer and zipped around the corner to the family room. He just stared at me for a few seconds, trying to recognize his daughter. In that few seconds his face went from scared half to death, to shock, and finally, to concern. At the end of his stare he tried to hide the tears in his eyes.

Dad had always been strong; no matter what the situation, he would fix it. He would do anything and everything to fix me. Mom took Dad aside, and I assume she filled him in. My uncle took my pressure again. To take the pressure, you use this gun-like machine and poke it straight in the center of the eye with the tip. This hurt like crazy, but the gun hitting my eye didn't hurt as much as trying to keep my eye open and looking straight ahead with the light, which was blinding, even though there was no light actually turned on in my kitchen or living room and it was dark outside. Blinding in this sense just meant another shock to my body, not actual vision because from the moment the smoothie lid hit my eye I had immediately lost all vision in my bad eye. This was the day I learned the power and pain of light—even the little amount left in my living room felt like torture.

My pressure was quite high and my uncle loaded up my eye with even more drops. Miles and his mom witnessed this, the beginning of the eye drops, and decided to head out and call it a night. It was getting very late, probably around midnight. Miles promised to tell my head coach and the other coaches what happened. He was going to call in the morning and see how I was. I told him I would drive down after I went to see the surgeon and Dad told Miles that he would personally drive me to OFSAA as soon as I was allowed.

Mom said that I probably wasn't going, but that just made me start crying and shaking and saying, 'I'm going, I'm going, I'm so sorry,' over and over again. Miles and his mom gave me a hug and wished me good luck. I would be facing some of the hardest few hours of my life.

As soon as they left, my uncle described the importance of sitting upright throughout the night. He also told my parents and me the seriousness of the injury, despite the way he had downplayed it for Miles and his mom. I felt completely traumatized by the fact that I might not be playing at OFSAA. I didn't really hear the blank words of truth that he told my parents.

The truth was that this might be more serious than any of us could have imagined. A badminton final in the next few days was the least of our worries because we needed to focus on the rest of my life. The truth was that I might not be able to see ever again from my right eye. The facts were painful and real. I wasn't just stuck in a nightmare.

My uncle told us the logistics: that I would need surgery in the morning and that the blood cavity could take months to drain. It would take a lot longer to drain then the blood blister Brianne had once gotten, which was the only instance of blood reabsorbing back into the body that I had ever known. Then he administered some more freezing and he left. It was getting late, and he needed to get home to his family. He thought I would remain stable for the next little bit at least.

Dad got me three more pillows and more of my teddy bears even though I didn't need them. I think he just occupied himself with physical tasks to distract his brain from the pain associated with the situation at hand. After all, men's brains are like waffles, compartmentalized, which only allows a man to focus on one thing at a time. By my dad focusing on the task to get pillows he didn't have to think about the pain or trauma that had just taken place.

Mom wouldn't leave my side. She got Dad to bring her pillow down to the couch so she could sleep there. This was the first of many, many sleepless nights we would spend together. Dr. Key dropped by again to check the pressure and give me more drops. We showed him the red-cap drop bottle my uncle had added to the collection and he agreed that we should keep administering it. Dr. Key left, saying the surgeon would call us and see me first thing in the morning.

    I stayed awake the rest of the minutes remaining in the night, replaying the incident over and over again in my brain. I kept replaying Miles' face when he saw me. I kept feeling like I had destroyed Miles and all of his dreams. I couldn't get comfortable or lie down flat. I just sat there wishing my brain would turn off, wishing I could wake up from this sleepless nightmare. Wishing I could think about something other than my dawning fate.

Pressure & Pain

*I'm sorry to say so
but, sadly, it's true
that Bang-ups
and Hang-ups
can happen to you.*

—Dr. Seuss

It was now 8:48 a.m. and I was counting down the hours until OFSAA began. I figured they would sew me back together and I would drive down and play with one eye. After all, we do have two eyes for a reason. Mom and I didn't sleep more than three minutes all night between contemplating the future, administering the eye drops, the immense pain, and worrying—let alone the fact that sitting upright with pillows shoved behind your head is not a position I will ever be able to fall asleep in no matter how tired I get.

The pain was still numbed to some extent by the shock I was in. I was in the greatest discomfort

I had ever experienced. Occasionally the shock would subside and I would feel the immense pain of my eye. It felt like my head was going to explode through my eye. I didn't realize that my eye had so much feeling in it. Apparently the eye is one of the most vulnerable pressure points on the human body. It is certainly the most exploitable on the face, but I still didn't understand how it could be so sensitive to such simple, normal things like light and movement.

Every millimeter I moved caused so much pressure it was almost unbearable. The few hours that some would call a night felt like eternity. The only blessing was the darkness that covered the house. At 5 a.m. Mom went for a quick shower and Dad sat with me. He was quiet as he just sat there watching me clench my fists in pain. I felt so weak I was thankful I could just sit in silence.

I was beginning to see how lucky I was to have such an amazing and caring family. What would have happened if I had been alone at home when it happened, or if I lived in rural Kenya, with no medical attention or numbing drops available? I appreciated each and every silent second I spent sitting with my father. My family surrounded me and loved me; I was the luckiest person in the world.

Carter and Brianne started to wake up. I don't know if they slept much either. Apparently I'm not the only one in the family who can't turn off their brain at night. They lay awake with worry most of the night, and I could tell by the slow movements and conversation they had that they were tired. I opened my left eye, the good eye, with all the might I had and saw a glimpse of dark circles under both of my siblings' eyes. Brianne went to school and Carter went to work at Toyota. Carter was on a work term this semester for co-op. I didn't realize how lucky I was that he was able to live at home. Dad went to work for a little bit, ready at any moment to leave once Mom called with the news that we were on our way to the surgeon's office.

Mom and I waited for the phone call from the surgeon, and the morning minutes ticked by more slowly than for any awkward or painful situation I had been in before. Mom kept herself busy trying to get a hold of my badminton coach. A bunch of my friends were leaving for the Algonquin trip that morning. None of them would know about my life-changing trauma as they went off to enjoy the wilderness. Mom just kept administering freezing drops, pressure drops, and pupil dilator drops to help soothe the pain.

Finally, around 9:00 a.m., Mom called the surgeon's office. They told me to come in right away. Apparently there had been a miscommunication with the three sources, Dr. Key's office, the surgeon's office, and me. Mom thought Dr. Key would call us in the morning when we should go, and Dr. Key thought he would hear from the surgeon's office as to when our appointment would be, but I guess the surgeon was just going to fit me in whenever I could get to her office. Despite the miscommunication, we were able to get going right away.

Dad was home in a jiffy and we were off to Dr. Ryann Squeel's office for the first time. I rode in the back seat of our car with lots of sunglasses and my hand held over my eye, trying to shield the light more. It was an odd feeling, wearing more than one pair of sunglasses, a feeling I didn't even notice due to the immense pain the light was causing me. The light just seemed to slip right through the sunglasses and even through my protecting hand. How was this possible? I had no idea, but it was only the beginning of my pain due to the power of light. We drove down a bunch of streets with way more bumps than I had ever noticed before. I couldn't tell you which streets we were on because both of my eyes remained closed. It was easier to keep my left eye closed as well.

Both eyes are connected, so you can't move one eye without the other. That's why it was easier for me to close my left eye too, so I wouldn't be moving my injured eye around and causing more pain to the lacerated eye. I could tell, however, that there were lots of lights and stopping and going, with every pebble causing extensive pain. It felt like my eye was splitting in half every time the slightest pebble caused the car to deviate from its linear path even a miniscule amount.

Dad offered to drop us off and we accepted graciously. He then drove through a parking gate and parked in a squishy parking lot. Dad was lucky to snag one of the last spots available. Mom and I ventured into the building through the glass doors. We clicked the elevator door and it was there almost instantly. We clicked the third floor button and even the light that comes on the button when you click it caused pain, even through my protective layers of sunglasses and my hand. Mom led me to Dr. Ryann's office. It was just to the right of the elevators. It was only two doors down, but with both my eyes closed holding onto my mom's arm, it felt a lot longer.

We entered the crowded waiting room and Mom led me to a seat, which somebody had graciously given up for me. The pressure difference from standing to sitting added a huge hurt to the already painful eye. Mom went to the desk and started filling out paperwork, but the secretary said to just do it later. This was urgent; Dr. Ryann would take me right away. The secretary led us around the desk and in the first room on the right. There were four rooms and four wooden doors in the wall. It was a very cozy office space, and I had no idea what to expect. I entered the office and was greeted by a pleasant brunette with a cool accent. She looked very nice, or at least she sounded nice. My eyes remained shut for the most part. I was led to a chair and sat down.

Dr. Ryann pried my eye open and put freezing drops in, and then she looked at my eye for twenty seconds. She looked up and asked two questions: 'Riley, are you eighteen?' I said that I was seventeen, and she said that she was going to waive the fact that I wasn't an adult. I found out later that this was so she could do the surgery herself and not have to fly me to a special unit for sick kids in Toronto. Her second question was, 'Have you had anything to eat in the last day?' Surprisingly, I hadn't; this was very odd for me and it was truly a miracle.

Then her voice got a little deeper and you could tell she was very serious as she said, 'Good, then, we're going into emergency surgery right now! I'll meet you at St. Mary's operating room, OR Four; go up the elevator and see the ladies at the desk. They will know you're coming. I will see you there!'

We were all in shock. After that news, Dad ran out ahead of us saying he'd get the car. As Mom led me out of the office I heard the bustle of secretaries calling and cancelling appointments. Dr. Ryann had just left a waiting room full of patients to do surgery on me! I didn't really realize I would need emergency surgery. I thought I had to wait for more blood to drain; I thought I would have time to prepare; I thought this was just a consult! I didn't really think about anything at the time, but looking back I realize I must have been in very rough shape for the head eye surgeon to leave an office full of desperate patients!

Surgery

Count backwards from twenty . . .

Dad sped to the hospital and we rushed up to the OR floor. Mom just led me; I couldn't have steered my way out of there if my life depended on it. Nothing consumed my thoughts besides the pain at this point—the agonizing pain of a hundred needles being stabbed into my eye and then splitting it apart. The freezing drops did absolutely nothing; they did not freeze my pain at all. It hurt so much I couldn't even think about anything else. I didn't have a chance to be scared or wonder what they were going to do to me. All I felt and thought was pain.

We went to the round desk, and I had to hold onto the desk to stay standing. I felt weak because of the immense pain I was in. A very nice nurse got me a wheelchair and made me sit in it. Mom told her that I was there for emergency surgery. The one lady was completely clueless, but then the boss girl came rushing in to take charge. She sent us downstairs to sign insurance forms and hospital mumbo jumbo. We went to the lobby, where Dad came running in to meet us. This nurse opened the welcome desk just for us, and when we finished, she closed it, apologizing to the people waiting in the room and saying she would come back. The nurse wanted to get me to surgery immediately so I actually had to sign waivers while being wheeled to the OR floor!

I was taken to a hospital bed where I was stripped and put in a gown. I kept my underwear on because the opening of the back was way too revealing for my liking. These actions would have normally made me very uncomfortable, especially since I hardly liked giving people hugs or others being in my personal bubble that always surrounded me. None of this mattered now, because self-conscious thinking didn't even fit in my brain because of how consumed with pain I was. I lay in the bed with the hospital blue engulfing me. The nurse took my blood pressure as we started moving. I love that feeling when the black cuff tightens around your arm and you feel your own heart beat. This was the only distracting sensation besides pain. This was the only thing I knew that meant I was alive. This rhythm comforted me and meant the pain wouldn't last. After all, pain is only temporary . . . right?

Next, the nurse put some stickers on my chest; the stickers felt freezing on my burning skin. I didn't realize how cold I felt or that I was shaking. The nurses seemed like a tag team, all doing different tests and prepping me for surgery. I just closed my eyes and lay there in silence, listening to my heartbeat and crying on the inside because the pain was drowning my voice, my movement, and my existence.

Soon I felt the prick of my IV needle, but it only felt like a tap on my shoulder compared to my pain—despite the fact that it took a few tries as they wiggled the needle around trying to find my veins. Next thing I knew we were picking up speed. The nurses were shouting 'Trauma victim OR Four, OR Four!!' I was like, 'Wow, that's so cool! I wonder what happened; I hope the person is okay.' Then I realized, as the doors to Operating Room Four opened, that I was the trauma victim. I was the one worth all this hustle and bustle. I was the character starring in this television show, except it wasn't a television show at all—it was my life.

I got into OR Four and opened my left eye, the uninjured eye, despite the pain I was in. I needed to see what was happening, plus the pain was only sharing my thoughts now because the IV had pumped me full of morphine. I saw all the scalpels and knives laid out on trays just like in the movies. I saw the flurry of people dressed in blue hospital cloaks with their hair tied back with colorful material, the blue plastic gloves, and the blue masks. I saw it all—every speck of blue, every sharpened knife, and every ready needle.

Then an old man with a creepy smile picked up a knife and said, 'Oh no, what happened here? Running with knives again?' I think he thought he was being funny, but I didn't even fake a smile to please him. I was just shocked. Then I saw Dr. Ryann and a wave of comfort came over me. She looked different in scrubs with a mask, but even though I had only seen her once before, I trusted her and was glad she was there.

Then a nurse gave me a form and asked if I had been prepped on the possible side effects . . . I looked up with my one eye struggling to remain open; I had no idea of the side effects—I didn't even know what I was having done to me! She just looked down at me and replied, 'Oh well, just sign and we can tell you after.' I couldn't tell you if I signed the paper or if my pen even lifted off the ground, but she seemed pleased with my efforts and left.

Then the nurse that had taken charge earlier and helped prep me and the nurse who had steered me like a race-car driver to OR Four reappeared. The second nurse had a soft face with a smile that reminded me of my grandma. She had short grey hair, pulled back now with froggy material. She told me, 'You're going to be all right, you're going into surgery now, try and count back from twenty . . .' Then I tried to count from twenty, but I'm sure it wasn't out loud because I didn't even hear the rest of what she said. I just knew it was beginning; they would be starting the first cuts. She was a very kind nurse and whether it was her words, and comforting smile or my faith that God was there for me, I knew everything would be all right.

Where am I?

*I am still determined to be cheerful and happy
in whatever situation I may be,
for I have also learned from experience
that the greater part of our happiness or misery
depends upon our dispositions,
and not upon our circumstances.*

—Martha Washington

I woke up six or seven hours later utterly confused. I felt like I was dreaming and just observing the things going on around me. There were nurses in the room, and there was an old man in a bed next to me. A nurse came right over and took some tests on me. All I wanted was to see my parents, but I couldn't find them anywhere. The nurse did so many tests it felt like eternity. After she finished, she just left me alone in confusion and disorientation.

I felt helpless. I was stuck in my dream observer state, unable to say anything. It was that same feeling you get while watching a sports game you really like and a sport that you play, like basketball or volleyball for me, and having no control in helping turn that two-point game around. It's like watching a game on the television and not actually being able to get up and join in the hustle and bustle. The difference was that this wasn't just a game I had no control over; this was my life. In the few minutes that felt like eternity, I started to panic. I realized how much I wanted my mom and dad and how much they meant to me.

The old man lying in the hospital bed beside me started talking to me. He asked why I was in the hospital, saying that I was too young to be here. I finally managed to mumble the words 'I have no idea.' He just continued right on talking and telling me that he had just had a heart attack and that the doctors were really good and had saved his life. The old man said that I would be all right and that he would make sure they took care of me too. He also pointed out that I had bandage all around my head and my right eye. He then just continued talking, telling me about his family, and once again I was thankful I didn't have to use all my energy to talk. As I half listened to this old man and half wondered why I was here and what had happened, my hand slowly raised to touch the bandage, clarifying what the man had said.

Then I saw the nurse with both my parents, and I instantly felt safe. The nurse sat me up because I was incapable of doing this on my own. Raising my hand to my head was enough of a challenge. She also made me eat crackers with peanut butter, although I was not hungry at all, which was a very strange feeling. Food had no purpose; I had no desire for it, even though a few days before I would have eaten an unlimited amount of peanut butter even if I wasn't hungry at all. It felt like there was no room in my stomach; I didn't even want the taste, which was so odd.

After I ate them I instantly felt like I was going to vomit, but I just swallowed it and nobody seemed to notice except the old man beside me. Mom and Dad were busy talking to the nurse. It felt eerily quiet and calm compared to our house. The only sounds were machines and the whispers of my parents and the nurse. I talked to the old man beside me once I could find the sound to go along with my voice. Apparently he had just gotten out of surgery too.

'Too?' That must mean I just had surgery. *Hmm, that's odd,* I thought. Nothing really hurt; quite frankly I couldn't even feel anything on my body. I kind of enjoyed that feeling. Mom and Dad finished talking to the nurse, and then they both put their arms on my legs and asked how I was. They said that Brianne and Carter had both called multiple times and were asking about me. I thought this was pretty cool, but still had no idea what was going on.

I had to wait overnight before I could be wheeled out to the car—if I remained stable. The night was honestly a blur. I just stayed in my same bed, but was wheeled to a room and Mom and Dad both stayed over just sleeping or sitting in chairs. I don't remember anything from that night and I feel like I almost time traveled into the next morning and the next day. The nurses continued to monitor the beeping machines and refill my IV, but aside from that I was just a vegetable sitting in a bed, unable to come up with enough strength to produce words. I felt exhausted, and I loved the feeling of sleep.

I woke up the next day around lunchtime, and the nurses allowed my parents to wheel me out to the car. I talked to possibly the nicest elderly man ever while waiting for Dad to get the car. He was so sincere; he said I wasn't allowed to get hurt because I had my whole life ahead of me. Mom explained what had happened to me, and for the first time vague memories started coming back.

At home we were greeted with Carter and Brianne's worried faces. Then I fell asleep in the deepest, most comfortable sleep of my life despite the fact that I was in that blue La-Z-Boy in an upright position. So much for believing that I would never be able to sleep in an upright position. Apparently circumstances change my abilities to do certain tasks and withstand things I never thought I could do.

Broken

> *When everything goes without*
> *a hitch where is the challenge*
> *the opportunity to*
> *find out what you're made of.*
>
> —Shania Twain

I woke up in the worst pain of my life. My eye wasn't just throbbing, it was burning. I wanted to rip it right out. I remembered being woken up throughout the night for eye drops, but it seemed kind of vague and dreamy. Mom came in and said I had an appointment with Dr. Ryann at 10:00 a.m. So I went to sit up more, but I couldn't because the pressure change in my eye was disastrous. It hurt so badly! The living room was completely dark, but I still felt like the sun had decided to shine right in my eye. I felt blinded and like I needed to cry, but I couldn't because it would just cause more pain. I couldn't even dry sob because the shaking caused too much pressure to my eye. I just closed my mouth and bit my lip. Turns out the colossal light was just my sister turning on the bathroom light behind closed doors on a completely different floor of our house. I was so sensitive to light I don't even know how to describe it.

In only a few hours I had lost all control of my body. I had no power, and I just had to trust in God that he would make things right. I knew I had loving parents who would take care of me and protect me. I went to Dr. Ryann with three pairs of sunglasses and two clenched fists. The standing and sitting and every bump in the car ride were torturous, but each task was something I could focus on to keep my mind off the pain.

We got to Dr. Ryanns' office and she had me go right in. I was getting lots of special treatment, but I guess that's because they treat the weak first. For once in my life I was the weakest link. I never want to be like that again. Dr. Ryann looked at my eye under the microscope. She had to put freezing drops in my eye and turn the light to the lowest, and it was still almost unbearable pain. I just wanted to push her away to prevent the added pain in my eye. She said it looked like the surgery had gone well, but that I would have to come back the next day to make sure I was stable.

I went home and welcomed sleep with open arms, although I had to be woken up constantly for eye drops. I was so exhausted that I had mastered sleeping upright in the La-Z-Boy. People came to visit and people called to see how I was doing. Honestly, the people were the only thing holding me on to reality.

The next few days were a combination of heavy-duty drugs like Percocet, visits to Dr. Ryann's office every day, drops every two hours throughout the night and day, friends calling and visiting, and sleep—oh, and most of all, pain. My sister would read my Facebook messages and e-mails just to distract me from the agony I was in. Brianne, Carter, Mom, and Dad spent hours with me just listening to the DVD player or music or reading to me.

Mom would respond to all my texts on my phone because I could no longer read anything or keep my 'good eye' open for more than a second at a time. I swear she became ten times better at texting those, hours, days, and weeks just because she had to. When you're faced with a situation, you just do it, even if all odds are against you.

I knew I would be okay and that God had a plan for me, and I knew that all this had happened for a reason. It was comforting knowing that God had our lives in his hands. I was still thinking and believing I was going to OFSAA, despite Dr. Ryann telling me otherwise. Dr. Ryann had switched her answer about OFSAA to 'maybe', just to keep me from losing control and going into another silent seizing and crying fit. I went home and resumed sleep in my newly claimed blue La-Z-Boy.

Mom tried to make me eat something, but I was too exhausted and too consumed by pain to even consider food. Food seemed so unappealing that I didn't want anything to do with it.

Anabeth came over that day. She just had her wisdom teeth out, so she understood how I couldn't eat when I was still on the drugs and with the anesthetic still in me.

Some of my friends from summer camp called because they had seen the Facebook update that Carter had written for me. It was so nice that even though they were far away they still cared. Both of my eyes now remained closed at all times because of the immense pain. If you move one eye, the other eye moves, so to protect my injured right eye, my left eye completely shut down.

I officially knew what it was like to be blind; to see nothing, to be in complete darkness 24/7. Being completely blind due to trauma is not like the black you see when you close your eyes at night. It isn't even that bright red colour when you close your eyes after being outside in the sun. I went from expecting colour and knowing what it looks like to not looking for anything at all—not seeing colour, but not expecting it either. For me, being blind was like me telling Brianne to see out of her pinkie toe, completely and utterly silly, unexpected, and impossible. Sight became unexpected despite the fact that a few hours ago, sight was all I would expect when I opened my eyes.

My thoughts and dreams were no longer in visual appearance. Everything I thought or "pictured" in my mind and memories were not pictures at all but audio. When I thought of an old memory it came to me with sounds to describe the events that had occurred. Pictures and visuals were as abstract as blindness had once been for me.

My other school and camp friends called, and it was so comforting. It was so much easier to talk over the phone than in person; I could mask my physical weakness over the phone. I could sound like I was doing okay and then, sleep the rest of the day to build enough strength to talk to another friend.

In spite of everything, I still had to decide on a school for next year, so my parents came into the living room and surrounded my blue La-Z-Boy and me. They laid out my options and said I needed to make a decision before the cutoff. I talked with my parents and narrowed my choices down to Western and Brock. They were the two options that were close so we could still deal with my eye problems if I needed appointments, and they were two programs I was really interested in. Western offered health science and Brock offered concurrent education to become a teacher.

I decided to flip a coin to decide my future. Heads was Brock and tails was Western. I knew that, despite the decision that was made, I would make the most of my first year and enjoy my decision either way. Dad had taught me that you can switch careers and jobs many times, so I knew I wouldn't be tied down. I got Carter to throw the coin up in the air . . . I could hear it spin a few times before landing with a thud. I asked him to read the coin and tell me what my future was. He said that it was heads; I would be a Brock Badger in no time. I was so relieved that the decision was made, it was like a huge weight had been lifted off my shoulders. I also felt confident with the decision.

My theory is that if you flip a coin and you aren't happy with the decision or the outcome, you just made up your mind to choose the other option. But this decision seemed to sit well with me, so I sent in the forms (well, my parents did), and I was officially accepted and hopefully going to Brock in the fall.

I received a phone call from Anabeth. She had found out I was going to Brock and asked to be my roommate. I also received a phone call from Brodie, who was on the Algonquin trip and hadn't even heard about my accident. I just laughed and acted like nothing was wrong. I told him the story like it wasn't actually affecting me, like it was a show that I had watched on TV. Through the phone I could pretend to be strong even though I felt like I was the weakest living organism out there, hardly alive at all. Despite my fake strength in these phone calls, I was completely drained afterwards.

When there were visitors I couldn't mask my tiredness. Occasionally I would fall asleep while I had visitors, and I would wake up to the sound of chatter and a wet pool of saliva that I had drooled during my nap.

My friends were superstars throughout my misery. Despite the fact that I fell asleep, it was the most welcoming feeling waking up to the sound of their voices, especially knowing that they weren't judging me for the pool of drool I had created. I will never forget each and every visit, flower, card, cookie, phone call, smile, thought, or prayer that I was given.

There is power in numbers and support, and without it I might have lost faith or hope or asked the question 'why me?', but because of all of the people who surrounded me every day, I stayed positive throughout the pain, stayed hopeful through the surgeries, and believed throughout it all.

This experience has given me a whole new perspective and appreciation for life. I would not have traded all the unbearable seconds for anything, knowing what I know now, seeing how much these situations have forced me and my family to grow.

New Ordinary

Human beings, by changing the inner attitudes of their minds, can change the outer aspects of their lives.

—William Jones

After the first doctor visit, I went back to Dr. Ryann's office almost every day. I got to know her as a kind and caring person with kids and a family of her own. She even put aside her family to make sure I was stable over the weekends. Due to the blood in my eye cavity taking time to reabsorb into my body, I would need to go to a specialist in London to check out my retina. Special equipment was needed to see the eye through all of the blood. The visits to Dr. Ryann's office seem like a blur because most of my days I was sleeping and drugged and in pain.

I think I tried to block out most of the painful memories to try and forget. I still remember that it was absolutely horrible, and I disliked not being able to worry about the little things like a bad mark, a bad outfit, or even the rain. I don't remember the exact feeling because it isn't possible to have the body go through that much pain again, but I do remember that it hurt, and it hurt bad; the pain was absolutely horrible and consumed my whole life.

Before this incident I was blind to a whole world that I neglected. My parents, friends, family, faith—these were things that I didn't even have eyes to see. Now I was blind to the things that used to consume me: school, what I looked like, boys, and most of all, my identity's core, sports.

Anabeth was amazing during these days of endless pain. She would come over often and even brought a special pillow to help me sit up because she knew I couldn't lie down. Dixon and Jonah brought me flowers and forced me to listen to their home videos as they explained through words what was going on. We all listened to *American Idol* together, and when the grounder boys came over they would take turns doing play by plays so I wouldn't miss anything by being blind. It was almost better coming up with my own ideas to what they were describing. I knew them so well that I knew exactly what they meant when they said, 'Now Dixon is shoving his face with cookies, but trying to do it with his back to us so nobody notices.' The grounder boys were helping me stay grounded despite our change in normal hangout activities. I was shocked that they actually came by and took a break from their active lifestyle to hang out and keep me comforted.

Brodie and his 'cool' friends even stopped by to see how I was doing. My youth group came and visited, and so many people flowered me with gifts, food, and cards. I will never forget the most heartfelt texts from the most random people.

I remember receiving a Facebook message from one of the 'bad kids' at our school. I mean like smoker pit, too cool to go to classes kind of boy. I didn't even think he knew I existed, let alone that he had a heart or cared for anybody. My sister Brianne read me this message that said, 'Hey Riley, I am so sorry I never said hi to you at school before. Your smile lights up our school and you seem like such a cool girl. I heard about what happened and I am so sorry. I will be thinking about you and hope you get better really fast. You are the last girl in the world to deserve this. I just wanted to let you know that you have really impacted our school and motivated me to be a better person. Let me know if I can do anything to help. Get better so we can see that smile back at school!' I was completely shocked! My heart just melted. I had no idea that I had made such a big impression before. I was getting notices and messages from people I didn't think knew I was alive.

I realized how important every decision, gesture, and action that we make is. I realized that people are influenced by your life whether or not you intend them to be. This made me realize I had the potential to help others and to make my school, my neighborhood, and the world a better place. This new perspective was very overwhelming, but also motivating, and I couldn't wait to hop out of my

La-Z-Boy and live my life with new purpose. What I didn't realize is that I wouldn't be hopping out of bed any time soon. I continued to be showered with love, shortbread cookies, flowers, visits, cards, texts, Facebook messages, and food. I was completely engulfed in love, pain, appointments, and darkness. Somehow being surrounded by love numbed the pain, or at least made it bearable.

Doctors

*Definition of doctor (noun): person who is
licensed to practice medicine.
My definition of doctor: my friends,
who I saw daily
who let me live vicariously through them.
Individuals
who knew me and cared for me
on many levels.*

I went to my usual appointment with Dr. Ryann. Her secretaries love me and my family. They always smile and ask how I am doing each and every day. I'm pretty sure it's because I'm the only one less than sixty years old in their office. Dr. Ryann's parking lot has huge speed bumps to get in and out of the lot. Each bump is added torture to my eye. We also have to pay each time we go in and there is a little drawbridge like arm that doesn't let us by unless we put our twoonie in. I bet half the money in that little collector box belongs to my mom and dad. A lot of the time Mom would drive me and

Dad would meet us there straight from work, so sometimes the machine would grab both Mom's and Dad's twoonie from us in one day.

After Dr. Ryann's 9:30 a.m. appointment we were off to London for a 3:00 p.m. appointment. Apparently this eye hospital was really good and the doctor there was excellent. Dad dropped us off and we went to sign in at the desk and answer all their questions. We grabbed some hand sanitizer and sat back down in the waiting room. This was the first time I'd had to wait since my eye incident happened, or at least wait in a hospital room where the staff wasn't all familiar and trying to sneak me in early.

After lots of waiting, we got situated into a smaller waiting room with interesting pictures of dogs in medical clothing or casts all over. A lady called me in and I went to an even tinier room, only big enough for me, Mom, this lady, and her machine. She opened my eye with this large metal clamp thing (my worst nightmare to this day). This was the first time I felt my eyelid being folded back like the blanket that it wasn't, but I was helpless to prevent the pain or do anything. It was worse than the scene from *Clockwork Orange* where the main character has his eyes clamped open as he is conditioned to perform violent acts.

Next she squirted this goop all over my eye and took an ultrasound. So much for ultrasounds being a pleasant experience at your first pregnancy with your perfect Prince Charming husband! I no longer like the idea of ever hearing that goop squirt out of that bottle or seeing that little ultrasound machine.

It hurt so bad. She was rubbing it right over my eye and occasionally she would get stuck on the stitches and her solution would be to just push harder. It was painful, and the nurse wasn't the most friendly person. I just squeezed my fingers and prayed it would end.

It was like having a knife wound, and then having somebody reopen it and rub it. I wasn't even able to get a video or picture of my eye like the baby ultrasounds. The lady was rude and hated her job, and by the way she treated my eye, she hated that, too. We went to a different waiting room and met some elderly folk. I just hope that the lady would have a better day the next day so nobody else would have to endure that unpleasant never-ending torture.

Dad made friends with all of the elderly folk. They were so nice and wise that I wondered what experiences they had been through to make them so kindhearted. I also wondered what I would be like when I was old. I then had a thought and heard myself speaking years from now sounding like a bullfrog. Yikes!

At last we got the chance to talk to the famous doctor. He was so friendly that he reminded me of my grandpa. He had a soft smile that comforted me. He asked me what had happened, and I replayed that moment that changed my life once again. He didn't grasp the smoothie bottle concept at first and he kept thinking that it was a beer cap, but he was a smart man and he eventually caught on.

He continued on to give me some positive news, telling me that my retina looked okay. Now, he didn't want to underplay the seriousness of my injury and the long road ahead would be filled with uncertainty and pain, but this was one positive step we all embraced. He also said he couldn't be 100 percent sure due to all the blood, but the ultrasound looked good.

Dad said goodbye to his new friends, I waved to the nice nurses in their colourful scrubs, and we left London with something positive to hold onto. I luckily didn't see the grumpy ultrasound lady, so our trip ended on a positive note. This was really the only sane thing keeping Mom and Dad together.

As soon as I got home, the rugby coach was there to visit. He gave me an original copy of a book filled with eye poems by a girl who had been in a similar situation. Each and every day I continue to be amazed by how much people care and how meaningful a simple gesture is. I wonder what it would have taken to change that ultrasound nurse's day around. I felt bad for not leaving her better off than when we went to her.

Torture

He who suffers much, will know much.

—Greek Proverb

May 21, 2011. I remember this date because it was the worst day of my life. My parents were going to celebrate their anniversary, and they were planning on going to see a Sting concert that evening. It was my first day without going to Dr. Ryann's office. This worried Dr. Ryann because if something was going wrong with my eye, she wouldn't be able to do anything to prevent it.

I had been on three drops every hour, administered ten minutes apart. That means only thirty minutes of no drops in a row. Thirty minutes is not enough time to accomplish anything, let alone get some sleep. I had been on these drops for multiple days now and there was no progress. At this point we had no idea what was wrong. I just knew that the healing process was not supposed to feel like this.

Round the clock eye drops meant no sleep at all for me as well as for the eyedropper, also known as Super Mom or any other volunteers that could be rounded up. So we were all exhausted, and Mom needed to go to this concert so she could realize that there was a world and a sky out there besides me and my agony.

My friend Anabeth had been interested in health science and enjoyed being an honorary eye-dropper. She did some practice ones while Mom was still home so Mom could supervise and provide her with tips as to how to hold the bottle. I had specific ways that my Mom had adopted that were the most comfortable and prevented some of the agony of the eye drops themselves. Then my parents were off to their concert.

At about 7:00 p.m., I began to reach my turning point. I was in extreme pain and I could not stand it. I was lying on the couch (my new home for the past few weeks) and I was being tortured. I was seizing, flailing, screaming into my pillow, crying with no tears.

The crying just made the pressure in my eye even worse. I honestly didn't know what to do with myself. Carter held my shoulders and arms down because he knew I was only hurting myself by flinging everywhere. Then came drop time. I felt like I was dying I was in so much pain. It was the closest I will ever get to Hell on earth. My brother did the drops because Anabeth didn't want to cause more pain. Carter knew that it had to be done. He sent the drop into my eye with one hand as he used his other hand to keep my eye open. The drop hit my lid, then burned and burned.

The memory of the pain still sends chills down my spine whenever I think about this horrific night. I moved up to my room for the first time since the accident. I needed to be in a bed instead of on a couch to help contain all my seizing. Mom had cleaned out all of my gym bags and my closet, but I made Brianne go ahead and make sure the door to the closet was closed. I had such an immense fear of my own room it was ridiculous. Something that had once been so comfortable and safe now left me terrified. My room used to protect me from the monsters under my bed, and now it had become the monster itself.

Brianne, Carter, and Anabeth took turns holding me down and reading Facebook messages and cards. This was usually the only thing that helped me, knowing that there was support out there. Tonight it didn't seem to help at all, and I told them all to watch the hockey game and just leave me alone. I didn't want to make their night any worse than it already was.

They must have felt so hopeless. They tried calling my parents, but Carter hung up on Anabeth's attempt and explained to them that my parents would be helpless in this situation also, so they should let them enjoy the few hours away from me they had. I remember there were no lights on because the light hurt me too much, and the only sound was the screaming that was coming from me. It was like it was straight out of a horror movie, except we couldn't hide behind the covers or turn this horror movie off.

* * *

Mom and Dad came home and found Carter, Brianne, and Anabeth in worried shambles. Anabeth went home and Mom and Dad came up to my room. They went into the hall where they thought I couldn't hear them, but due to my blindness I had heightened senses and heard every word.

Dad begged to be allowed to give me another Percocet (pain pill). Mom said no and that it wouldn't help in the long run. She said that we weren't allowed, and that we should be following doctor's orders right now. She didn't want me to become addicted or develop any further problems.

The worst part about being in this unspeakable state, unable to create actions for yourself, is that people think you can't hear or see by the sounds, but even though my eyes were blind, I could see how everything played out in my head. Mom and Dad were screaming at each other over me. I had never heard either of them full out yell before. It was completely my fault, and I couldn't do anything about it. I had spread this helpless feeling from not only myself, but to my parents.

Once my parents had calmed down and taken out their anger on one another, I heard their footsteps enter my room. My parents were both crying and took turns sitting with me holding me.

Dad even cried and held my leg; he never shows his love through actions like putting a comforting hand on me, but the pain I was in seemed to break his protective bubble. Besides an occasional awkward, forced hug, he was a very unemotional guy, but the pain just seemed to break that barrier.

Mom was sitting with me sometime around 3:26 a.m., and I say sitting because it does not count as sleep when you are propped so high by six pillows that the blood will drain/reabsorb. There is a point when your body and mind are completely absorbed with pain that even though you wish to sleep, it is not physically possible. I could not sleep due to pain and Mom could not sleep due to being consumed with worry. I was in the most pain I have ever felt, and I grabbed her hand and said, 'Mom, can you please just kill me? I would rather be dead in Heaven than feel this.' It was the lowest point of my life.

We made it until morning. Mom never left me; she just prayed and prayed that I would be able to bear the unbearable for the rest of the night. Never have I felt such hopelessness. Life without hope is torture.

Help

None of us has gotten where we are solely by pulling ourselves up from our own bootstraps. We got here because somebody bent down and helped us.

—Thurgood Marshall

The next morning I went back to Dr. Ryann's and she appeared to be really worried. What we thought was a bacterial infection was still growing despite the drops. She cut one stitch right there in her office, with no pain meds or sedation. It felt like a pointy, rough snake was being pulled from my insides and out my eye. It was a sickening feeling, like when you feel naked because you're not wearing your watch or a ring that you normally wear. It was such a strange feeling, but it wasn't as painful as the night before. plus there was the hope that this would help. That seemed to override the pain for the moment.

She took the stitch out in the hopes that the drops would be able to reach deeper into my eye to kill the infection. We went home to try this plan of action. It seemed pretty odd to open up the cut again. Dr. Ryann called our home number, telling us that she had booked an appointment at a Toronto hospital with her old boss. The Toronto hospital is about an hour and a half car ride from our home without traffic. She told us she didn't know why my eye was getting worse, but that they would be able to figure it out.

We got home and realized that we had mail from the insurance company. We braced ourselves for the letter saying that they couldn't cover the eye drop expenses. But to our surprise the letter said that the $7.00 insurance plan from Billa-Aid High School covered the eye drops! That's right, all the millions of bottles were covered. Sometimes one eye drop bottle was over $600.00 because it had to be shipped from California! It was our first of many miracles.

Our whole family was so excited that Mom decided to make a huge dinner. She called us all to the dinner table (even me getting up from my home on the couch). I had to be led to my seat at the table because I was still completely blind. Although I was completely blind, I could sense the light and therefore all the lights, aside from a small candle, were turned off. I wasn't the only one in darkness; I had forced my whole family to endure this dark fate as well.

Once we were sitting at the table, Mom relaxed and went to serve our celebration meal. Then as she went to scoop out the potatoes, my sister Brianne goes 'Mom, these potatoes are cold . . . the stove isn't even on.' Mom had officially gone crazy due to lack of sleep. Apparently eye drops every hour does that to people; no sleep is a hard lifestyle. I remembered being overtired because of all the sports and activities I used to do, but this was pure exhaustion. I vowed to never complain of lack of sleep ever again after this! Needless to say, we ordered a pizza.

Hope

Hope is all it takes to get through another day.

*"For I know the plans I have for you," says the Lord.
"They are plans for good and not for disaster,
to give you a future and a hope."
—Jeremiah 29:11*

We left for Toronto at 5:00 a.m. the next morning, which was a blessing because it meant that the painful night of silence, no visits, and nothing but drops would be shorter. Nighttime was the worst time for me because there weren't people distracting me from the pain. There was only silence. It was the first of many daily visits and overnight stays to see Dr. Hank Wisdom and all the Toronto hospital staff.

When we got there, Dad dropped us off, and Mom led me to the elevator on the sixth floor. The elevator's pressure change bothered my eye; it hurt so much! Even going to the bathroom was something that caused pressure in my eye and hurt too much to do. I remember people in school joking that once Brodie's face looked constipated because he was trying so hard on a math question, and I now realized the pressure in tasks such as going to the bathroom. Worse, the pressure was extremely amplified now. Brodie's pressure, shown in his face if he was constipated, for me felt ten times worse even when I was going to pee. Bending down to sit on the toilet and straining my face was brutal. Simple tasks like putting on socks or changing became difficult or impossible. I hardly went to the bathroom anymore, but that wasn't a problem because I was not eating anything due to the medication. I was slowly shriveling up into a true vegetable.

We walked to the sign-in desk, registered, and waited. Mark, a big black Jamaican man, got up and we were led to Room Seven. There was room for both of my parents in there. It was comfortable and filled with machines and tools.

Dr. Wisdom turned off the light so it didn't hurt me as much. Then he said that one of his fellows would perform an eye biopsy. I met Dr. Cheme, a fellow, for the first time, and then I was led to a surgery room where I took off my Birkenstocks and lay down on the surgery bed. They strapped me down, and I knew I was in for something serious. Dad needed to leave the room because the look of the tools didn't settle too well with his stomach.

Mom decided to stay, and she sat down on a stool so she could hold my hands throughout the surgery. I am pretty sure I squeezed her hand so tight that I could have broken her fingers. I squeezed harder than I ever thought humanly possible. A bigger, friendly nurse asked Dr. Cheme if she needed her to stay. I said, 'Yes, please', thinking that she was asking me. She already felt like a friend and I trusted her. She just giggled and Dr. Cheme replied, 'I guess we have our answer, Riley wants you to stay. Can you grab that tray for me?'

Dr. Cheme adjusted the straps holding me to the table and tightened them before moving to my head. The straps were up and down the table and me, holding me in place, preventing any movement. She used the clamp that I hated so much to open my eye and fold my eyelids back like a blanket. Then she cut open my already sliced eye, grabbed a needle, and scraped some of the unknown organism growing in my eye into a vial. She had to fill six vials, and I asked if she could try and just scrape it all off. She said that that would ruin my eye in the long run, causing too much scarring for me to ever have a chance of seeing again.

During the scraping process I sneezed twice and Dr. Cheme screamed! She was scared she went through my eye and hit something deeper. I had to be conscious during this procedure, and I did not like it one bit. I would much rather be completely out of it, back on Cloud Nine. It was a scary moment when she screamed, but she resumed surgery and was confident she didn't hit anything.

I had to be awake for this surgery because she was sticking needles in my eye and she wanted to make sure that I remained conscious so they didn't hit anything too deep. I wasn't on pain pills anymore because I had been switching from hospital to hospital and they didn't want to overdose me. The only thing keeping me sane was the freezing drops they put in my eye, but those hardly froze out any of the pain at all.

They unstrapped me from the deathbed and the pain just got worse. It hurt to sit up, and then standing was even more painful. They decided that I had to stay in this hospital and be put on pain pills right away.

I got prescribed heavy drugs so I would feel like I was on a cloud. We had to go home to get all of our belongings and check back with Dr. Ryann, and then I would return to the Toronto hospital as an in-patient. The car ride home was rough; I had never noticed all the bumps on the roads before. The medication set in once we got half way home, and I felt like I was floating above my life, a pleasant change to living in agony.

The doctors at the Toronto hospital were like the ones on *Grey's Anatomy*, with fellows under the surgeons. There were doctor's orders, drama, and mayhem to go right along with the show. Little did I know that I would be getting a front row seat to their lives because I would have to stay in Toronto for a large chunk of my life to this point.

Dad took huge chunks of time off work just to visit me, and he witnessed Dr. Wisdom and his daily appointments and booster juice. Dr. Wisdom drank a booster juice every day after he completed the morning surgeries.

Home

*Life doesn't suck ever
it's always just a journey
parts are painful
but when the pain goes you realize that
it didn't suck
it's just life
it's a beautiful mess.*

—Brendan Barrack

My parents returned to the Toronto hospital to see me for the third day in a row. Some nights Mom would just stay over and sit with me. She had to quit her job being an occasional teacher because she wanted to do everything she could for me. Dad would drive up every day and had to sacrifice his job and sleep just to be there for me. My brother and sister would call me every day and so did my friends and extended family.

I seemed to be getting more and more excited for Miles' daily phone call. He made me feel like I wasn't an incapable athlete. He made me feel like we would still be going to OFSAA and that part of my life was just on pause. Although in reality it had been going on while I was a vegetable in hospitals all over Ontario. With the combination of pain medication and talking to Miles, I felt like I was on Cloud Nine all the time.

They had the eye biopsy results in and ready. They found out that I had a deep fungal corneal ulcer. A fungal infection is more spectacular than you may think; they are far less common than bacterial infections. In fact, out of all the doctors I had seen, Dr. Wisdom was the only one who had seen one in his life. He was also the best eye doctor in all of Canada. He was the head honcho and a big deal when it came to eyes. Some argued that he was one of the best in the world!

Fungal infections (Fungal Keratitis) were rare and very hard to treat. Dr. Wisdom explained how, if they had tried to scrape the complete fungal infection off with the eye biopsy (or culture, as they say in medical terms), it would just come back. I now had a hypopyon in my eye as well. A hypopyon is a big pus-ugly thing that covered the majority of my eye except for the fungus and sliced area. I had the most attractive eye in the world . . . NOT!

I was getting to know the Toronto hospital as my new home. I was comfortable here and the doctors were my new best friends; after all, I talked to them all the time. Dad began to warm up to Mark, who at first he thought was very cold and mean because Mark was in charge of taking my pressure. Dad thought this looked like a horribly painful procedure, but actually they put freezing drops in and it wasn't as bad as it looked. He used a machine with a pointy needle-like end to poke the middle of my eye. It didn't actually hurt too much because my eye was normally frozen, although you could still feel something even if it wasn't pain. I would feel changes when I was poked. With some of the pressure machines you didn't even have to touch the machine to the eye, but majority of the time it happened by accident anyway.

The nurses would tell me about their boy problems, their children, sisters' weddings, and bring in pictures to show my parents and fill me in. The day we got the eye biopsy results was the day I could begin to open my left eye, the one that hadn't been lacerated by the smoothie lid. I was no longer a prisoner to this darkness and world of sound. The pictures they brought in were motivation for me to try to keep my left eye open long enough to try and make out these pictures.

It was the most amazing thing ever to be able to see again. It wasn't gradual; it was just like I expected—nothing one minute, and the next I could see. I could see colour, texture, shading, shadows, lights, and darks! Even if it was only for quick blinks, it was the most amazing experience of my life. I have no idea how somebody couldn't believe in a God after going from being blind to seeing again. The beauty and literal 'awe' that I was in was preposterous. Each object had a new meaning and purpose. Sight is a beautiful thing, and I couldn't look at everything quickly enough. I was just stunned with the breathtaking view of the hospital room. Those blue footcover slippers, the blue sheets on the bed . . . how was it possible that there were so many different blues?

My good uninjured eye got tired very quickly and closed again, but the difference in closing my eye now was that it was black, like when you close your eyes to sleep. There was something there, even if my eye wasn't open. I knew that this was going to be a great start to a new perspective and appreciation for sight and life itself.

Just a few minutes after this beautiful discovery, I heard the telephone ring. Mom was conked out and taking a power nap beside me, so I reached over and picked the phone up. It was Curly, my badminton coach. She had called to tell me that I had won the True Billa-Aid award! The award for top female athlete! I had not been to Billa-Aid in weeks. My life had been transformed full of new perspectives, priorities, and purpose. I hadn't even thought about the pressures of awards and competition that was going on at Billa-Aid.

It's strange how one week you're stressing over tests and who your date to prom will be, and the next day none of that matters and you don't know if you'll ever be able to live a normal life again, ever be able to see again. It's crazy how much stress we put on ourselves over silly things and how whacked our priorities are. I wished that I had appreciated sight more before the accident, especially if I would now be blind forever. What would have happened if I hadn't opened my good eye today and had never taken the time to appreciate the beauty in the world? I would have bypassed a magnificent part of life. We take so many silly little things for granted—even reading people's faces when we talk to them.

Anyway, I said that I would be able to go to the athletic banquet, and I would give a speech. I then had to convince the doctors and the nurses to let me go home for the banquet. I really wanted to be a part of Billa-Aid and not be the one to miss out on a memory that was taking place. It was hard missing out on the events that all my friends would be talking about.

Today was a great day. I could actually see again, and I had been awarded one of the best honours in our whole entire school! I just had to convince Mom and the doctors to let me back to reality for one day.

After lots of begging and notes that I would leave on my food trays, the doctors and nurses finally agreed and said that Mom would be able to do the hourly drops so I would be allowed to go home. I would be travelling back to reality, and I wondered if it had stayed the same or changed as much as I had.

Athletic Banquet

I believe in pink.
I believe that laughing is the best calorie burner.
I believe in kissing, kissing a lot.
I believe in being strong when everything seems to be going wrong.
I believe that happy girls are the prettiest girls.
I believe that tomorrow is another day and I believe in miracles.

—Audrey Hepburn

I returned home the next day, promising that I would make the trip to the Toronto hospital every other day for appointments with Dr. Wisdom. The drops seemed to be working a little bit and I was at least stable.

Dixon came over to my house and helped me with my speech. He was an awesome friend. Curly and a few of the teachers from Billa-Aid dropped off an audio book so I could feel more like a human and listen to something while laying in bed. Turns out the book was about a girl who goes blind and learns to cope with the change. The teachers didn't do this on purpose, although I got a good laugh when Curly brought it over. I had received some other presents from my classmates and my homeroom teacher had actually made a CD with a song from each student in the class. I had the best people in the world surrounding me! A few months ago I had had no idea I was the luckiest person in the world. I felt like I was being spoiled, and my friends, family, and community that surrounded me brought me through the pain and were a huge distraction from my helplessness.

It was interesting to see how each person showed their support in a different manor. Some brought over gifts and presents, others spent time with me, some spoiled me with encouraging words, some would try and give me hugs or hold my hand and others would complete acts of service for me that I could no longer due. It was neat to see how everybody around me worked in such unique ways.

The night of the athletic banquet approached faster than I expected. Before I knew it, it was the night I was waiting for. The athletic banquet is a formal event, and I would have to shower and look nice, which was a task I had not completed in quite some time. I asked Mom and Brianne if they had any idea of a dress I could wear. I had lost a lot of weight and wasn't sure if anything would fit me.

Brianne found a dress I had bought earlier that year and said it would be perfect. Surprisingly, later that night, it proved its use and magically still fit.

Then Mom pulled some strings and got me into my hair dressers to wash and dry my hair. I couldn't shower for the fear of getting my eye wet, and I couldn't wash my hair in a bath without excruciating pain. Plus I felt like baths were like swimming in your own gook and I spent as little time in there as possible. Dad drove me to the hair dresser and they brought me to the back of the studio where it was dark. They washed my hair with extreme care and they made it fast because I had zero strength to even sit in the chair without help without falling over. My hair was clean for the first time in way too many days, and I returned home for my exciting evening.

When we got home I had a nap to build energy for the big night. I woke up and threw the black dress on. I realized I had backne (acne on your back) for the first time in my life. It's strange how different situations change your body; you don't realize what you used to take for granted. I was in no state to care and was just excited that I was allowed out of the house for something other than going to the hospital.

I had to wear an eye patch to help block out the light. This was the first event I would be at, and I knew I would be making a fashion statement. I also knew that people would be staring. It was a new concept to get used to, people staring at me and wondering what was wrong.

I got dropped off to the closest door to the cafeteria where the banquet was being held, where I was met by Anabeth, Dixon, Jonah and Miles. They all escorted me to a seat they had saved at the senior students' table. We had finally earned the seniority to sit at the front table. Many people gathered around me and asked how I was and about a thousand other questions. It was nice to know that people cared about me, and I loved answering questions and clearing up any confusion. It was interesting hearing the stories of what people had heard. Apparently I had been in a knife fight, tripped out of the shower and landed on scissors, got in a car crash, and wrestled a bear. It was sad denying all these stories and admitting to being beat up by a smoothie bottle, but it was amusing all the same.

People were standing all around before the banquet began and taking pictures. The flash hurt so much I couldn't bear it, so I just stayed put at our table with my head down in my arms. Plus the walk into the cafeteria just about drained me, and I hardly had any energy left. I attempted to be in one picture and my good eye couldn't even remain open for the split second it took to take the picture, and my bum eye just throbbed in pain even though there wasn't a flash.

Finally the questions stopped coming and the banquet began. I had Anabeth on one side and Jonah sitting on my other side. Miles was sitting at the head table because he was athletic rep. It gave me goose bumps just looking at him. It was crazy, but amidst the health issues and simplicity of my recent life, having this little schoolgirl crush made me feel sane. Sure, my priorities had changed and I now took life with so much more appreciation. I loved my family every second and realized the importance of certain things, but this crush just wasn't going away despite the trauma.

I just about instantly fell asleep and started drooling. Good thing Jonah woke me up when I won some MVPs and honourable mention awards. My teammates who won awards around the time I was called would take the time to help walk me up to accept the award and walk me back. Mom would also sneak up the aisles and put eye drops in for me during the banquet.

It felt so surreal to be back at Billa-Aid being recognized for sports that felt like a lifetime ago. It was amazing to be recognized at all, and I had gone into the banquet with a gut feeling that I would have been forgotten since I hadn't been there in so long. I felt like such an oddball out, and it was nice to be supported and loved in such a manner.

Each time I returned from collecting an award, I fell asleep again. Before I knew it, it was time for the major awards. It was neat to see my friends go up and give speeches. Of course, 'see' is a relative term in my case. When you listen to a speech or your surroundings, you actually get a lot out of it by visualizing the scenario to tell what's going on. Now that my sight had come back in my good eye, even if I couldn't keep it open to watch my friends speeches my ideas of what was going on around me formed a visual picture in my mind instead of an auditory one.

Once the major award section began, Jonah woke me up and wiped the crusted dried drool from my face. I smiled and thanked him; I was truly grateful for my friends and the things they would do for me. Then I was instantly awake and no longer tired because the swarm of butterflies in my stomach had been awakened too. They were going crazy; it felt like I had a whole family in there. It was the moment I had been anticipating. Jonah had won an award where he was introduced but didn't get to say a speech, and the coach had joked about how he had run during the swimming portion of a triathlon. Apparently he had run on the bottom of the pool and been given a five-minute penalty.

It was hard to hear stories about times I couldn't be a part of. It was my worst fear, missing out on events, moments, and people while I was stuck in my sleepy, medicated, fragile state. I was determined that after I was better (because I was going to get better), I would do everything I could. I would meet everybody I had the chance to, just because each and every person out there has the potential to change my world and I can't risk not getting that opportunity. I didn't really have time to think about this life-changing view until later because the butterflies were going crazy and I felt sick.

Curly walked up to the stage and started describing the award I was supposed to receive: the True Billa-Aid award. I started wondering if maybe it was a cruel joke. Maybe I didn't actually win at all, maybe they made a mistake and read my name because it was actually the person above me alphabetically. The possibilities for it not to be me were endless, and each and every option was running through my head. Curly described the award as being given to a very deserving recipient, one who not only demonstrated the top athletic ability throughout her high school career in a number of different sports, but also did it with passion, kindness, selfless leadership, and a number of other qualities that I couldn't even hear because I was sure it wasn't me and they had made a mistake.

Then my head took a wild spin as I heard my name. Curly announced into the microphone for the whole banquet to hear, "I would like to welcome Riley to the stage!" The crowd went wild as I walked up to the stage with my paper full of point form notes scribbled on it. I stood by the side of the podium as Curly continued to commend me on my years and the inspirational moments I had put in at Billa-Aid. I no longer heard anything she said as my brain was trying to grasp the reality of the situation. I had won this incredible award that I only dreamed about, and it wasn't a dream. I was in shock, but it was so different from the shock when that smoothie bottle exploded. The crowd started clapping. and I realized it was my turn to go up to that dreaded podium.

I gave Curly a huge hug and thanked her with that deer-eyed shocked look on my face, and then I stepped up to the podium. My eyes were closed and it took a huge amount of strength to attempt to open my left eye slightly. As I did, I saw all the faces of my friends and classmates, the athletes that I had strived to be just like, all looking out and staring at me. Instantly comforted by their faces, I put my right hand up over the shield to block out the excess light that was sneaking through the cracks, and I took a big long breath.

Then I just started talking.

'So I have no idea why I brought this paper with notes on it anyway. I can't really see anything, let alone read it. I'm sorry I couldn't write out an amazing articulate speech, but everything I am going to say is coming right from me and I mean each and every word sincerely.'

I went on, 'Wow. Wow, I cannot believe this is real. I remember when I was sitting in that back corner listening to those big, scary superstar athletes passing on their wisdom to me. I remember thinking and wishing to one day be just like them. I am so honored to be standing up here right now and just in complete shock. Thank you so much!

'I would like to start by thanking my coaches to the extent that they deserve, but that just isn't possible. I couldn't thank each and every one of the individuals for all the seconds, minutes, and hours of time they have spent on me. They have created so many inspirational and memorable moments that have created motivation and drive for my fellow teammates and me. Each coach that I have been lucky enough to have has passed some of his or her wisdom on to me. Each one is so amazing and I appreciate all the hard work and knowledge you have passed on. Thank you so much for investing in me.'

Even though I couldn't see, I tilted my head toward the table where my friends and family sat. 'I would also like to thank my friends and family. First of all, I would like to say that I must be the luckiest person in the world. As most of you can see, I have a pretty cool eye patch covering my right eye. Well, I know you are all thinking, "Wow this girl has style", but let me tell you it's not just a fashion statement.' The crowd erupted into laughter, and I was so surprised somebody thought I was funny. I went on. 'A few weeks ago I was packing my bag for OFSAA and a smoothie bottle exploded, leaving my life completely changed.'

I could hardly finish the sentence without getting all teary in my one eye even though it was closed. I had that feeling in my nose like somebody is squeezing out a sponge, but it's actually the top of your nose and you just have to resist; otherwise the waterworks and crying will start.

I took a breath and continue. 'I realized that I had the most loving and caring family in the whole world. They loved me so much and would literally do anything for me. My brother Carter has helped put eye drops in and make me laugh when it feels like the world is coming to an end, Dad has risked the future of his business to take days off to drive me to hospital after hospital, my Mom is a freakin' superhero. She has put eye drops in every hour for what seems like most of my life. She is even here tonight, sneaking in to give me eye drops throughout the banquet, and last but not least, there is my sister Brianne. Umm, she is good for something, but I just can't . . . I'm kidding—she spends time with me, and she reads my Facebook messages and texts from all of my friends to help show me that I am not alone in the world and to show me that I have people pulling me out of this pain. I love my family immensely and this incident has shown me that I cannot take them for granted; They have really made me a priority and I will always do the same for them.

'This incident has also shown me that I am the luckiest person in the world because it has opened my eyes (not literally... well, not yet, at least) to all the amazing friends I have. My friends have been incredible, and I can say from the bottom of my heart that they have pulled me through this. If it wasn't for them I honestly do not know what would have happened. They are so important in my life. I would especially like to thank my badminton partner, Miles. I am so sorry I had to crush your dreams at OFSAA and . . .' I couldn't finish my sentence because I burst into loud, uncontrollable tears. It was the most unattractive thing ever. I was shaking and sobbing, which just hurt my eye more, which I had temporarily put on the back burner of my brain. Miles came up to the podium and gave me a huge hug. He was crying his eyes out and so was most of the crowd. He was sitting right beside the podium at the head table because of his emceeing position as athletic rep.

He said. 'Riley, don't be sorry, you are an inspiration. I am just happy you're okay,' then he said it, with the trail of his voice caught by the mike . . . 'Riley, I love you.' He continued to comfort me, and then I stopped shaking and just skipped over what he said in my brain. There wasn't even time to fathom that, I had a speech to finish. He told me to keep going. 'You can do it, Riley.' I stepped back up to the podium and continued

'Sorry about that; I blame the happy pills I'm on. Apparently they make me sad too.' The crowd burst into laughter even though some were still drying their eyes from the tears they had cried when I was addressing Miles. It was incredible the crowd was experiencing the same emotions I was. I was actually getting across to them!

'I should probably wrap it up because you are all probably bored out of your minds, but I would just like to stress the importance of the relationships you build here. May it be side by side on the court or sitting next to somebody warming that bench, trust me, I've been in both spots. Each moment you spend with these people has the potential to change your life and change the world. Sports are great and I love them deeply, but they aren't who you are. I realized that these past few weeks—the sports and skills aren't what make me Riley. It's the people who create these memories and laughter. I am going to remember the people . . . and the moment when Anabeth scored that winning shot. I won't remember the sport. That is why sports carry different meaning and memories for each and every one of us sitting here today. When I am laying in bed, basketball isn't going to come give me a hug to keep me going—you guys are!

'I would also like to leave you with the biggest lesson I learned this year. We are not invincible. We are not going to live forever, and we have no idea what is going to happen. So take advantage of each second you do have with your friends, each second you are able to run that sprint or soak up the wisdom from your coach. Soak up as much from life as you can and remember that you are impacting every single person around you. Make that impact a positive one and use sports to help you create those relationships and moments you will never forget. I have no idea what will happen, but I do know that sometimes we do have control and we have the choice to give it 100 percent, so when we do have control we should make the best of every second, try our best, and succeed.'

By this point I had burst into tears again and couldn't really talk, but it didn't even matter because when I looked up through my squinted left eye, I saw that the whole crowd was on their feet crying and clapping! Each and every person in the cafeteria had wet cheeks from crying, even the tough football boys and my grounder boys. Even Brodie and all of his cool friends were crying. I looked to the back where my parents were standing, Mom with the eye drop lunch bag in hand and Dad wiping his eyes because he, too, was crying. I had made Dad cry and discovered that teachers I didn't even know had hearts. It was like I had been blanketed with a wave of gratitude and appreciation as I looked out and saw all the lives I had touched. The standing ovation was the first and last of the night, and it just proved to me that being real and being honest is appreciated. My speech was real and touching and made even the tough, heartless football guys cry. I went home knowing I was truthful and real on my one night out, even if I fell asleep on the car ride home.

After the banquet was done I was exhausted, but I wanted to talk to each and every person there and tell him or her how he or she had influenced my life. I talked with all of my coaches and teammates, and we reminisced over different funny moments. We also discussed how life goes on after sports and how I was doing with my eye. For one night I felt like I was getting attention because of my achievements and not because of my accident. I was too exhausted to move, but then Brodie came up and gave me the nicest compliment I have ever received. He went on about how I was so inspirational and how each and every day he tried to be as positive and as nice as me. I was so shocked and amazed at how much I was appreciated. I knew that he would have been just as amazing if the smoothie had exploded in his face.

    Then Miles helped carry me to the car because I could no longer walk. I fell asleep in his arms and just barely woke up as he buckled me into the back seat of my parents' car under the big starry sky in the Billa-Aid parking lot. I don't know what he said because I was instantly asleep, and I don't remember anything else from that night. One thing I do know is I went to sleep with a big goofy smile plastered on my face.

Reality

*I'm not a perfect girl
my hair never stays in place
I spill things, a lot
I'm clumsy
and sometimes have a broken heart
my friends and I fight
some days nothing goes right
but when I think about it
and take a step back
I remember how truly amazing life is
and that maybe,
just maybe I like being
imperfect.*

- Luna

I woke up the next morning not knowing what was real and what had been a dream. The athletic banquet had felt so surreal and perfect that it was hard to grasp the reality of it all. I bet if I had more energy I would have just stayed awake because, for once in my life, reality was way better than any dream I could ever come up with, even better than those crazy dreams you have when you're on Percocet.

I was absolutely exhausted and just laying in bed letting the athletic banquet night sink in. I had no energy to do anything, and I couldn't even sit up for visitors. The banquet had drained me, but it was totally worth being completely exhausted if it meant I got to enjoy a night like that.

I was repeating the events of the evening over and over in my mind, and I just smiled to myself thinking about how my friends had taken care of me. I smiled at the thought that Dixon had won the male version of my award. It made it even more special to share it with such a good friend. Then I remembered the moment when Miles said that he loved me!

Wow. This was hard to grasp. There are just so many different meanings of the word love. Like, did he mean he loved me like he loves cheese, or that he loved me like a friend he wants to stay in touch with, or love like a sister? Then there was the possibility that he loved me as more than all of those things, the possibility that he was feeling the electric shock I felt when we touched. Maybe I consumed all of his thoughts too, and he couldn't focus on anything without relating it to me. Then maybe I was just delusional because of the drugs. Who would want to have a crush on a blind girl?

Then it hit me that prom was coming up. It was my grade twelve year and that meant I would only have one shot at prom. So many questions popped into my head. Would everybody forget about me? Would anybody even want to ask me to prom when they would be on eye drop duty for sure? Who would want a date who has to wear an eye patch and potentially can't shower? Wow. I realized I was doomed.

I had bought my prom dress a few months earlier because I found a gorgeous one on sale. I had no idea if it would still fit, let alone look half decent. At the next hourly eye drop session I told Mom that I wanted to try it on. She dug the dress out of her closet. I stayed well away because any closet still traumatized me. She then helped me put it on. It was a miracle. The dress fit perfectly, as if I had bought it yesterday. I turned to her and asked her if I was actually seeing and feeling it correctly. She smiled a big ridiculous Mom smile and said, 'Riley, you look more beautiful than ever, and it fits absolutely perfectly. I have no idea how, but it does. It looks perfect.'

Mom doesn't use the word perfect too often so I knew it had to look okay. I was then worried that maybe it was a Mom opinion and not a valid cool, teenage opinion. I called Anabeth and she was soon on her way for a second opinion. It passed Anabeth's approval—she loved it too!

It was a bold dress and I hadn't known if I could pull something like it off before when I blended in. Now I was even more worried I would stick out like a sore thumb and look bad doing it. The mini fashion show made me a little more confident, but I still didn't have shoes or a purse.

Mom said she would go shopping the next day while Anabeth came over and took over drop duty. Mom would pick something out. I had to fully rely on Mom, and that scared me a little when it came to fashion. I really had no other option, though, because going to a mall was out of the question.

I continued my every-other-day Toronto hospital visits and the staff were becoming more like family. I felt at home when I walked through those automatic hospital doors. Dr. Cheme asked me to bring in my award and pictures from the athletic banquet. All the doctors commended me and came to hear all about the night. Mark was a huge support, and I couldn't help but become fast friends. Dad had even softened up on Mark despite him having to poke me in the eye to check my pressure. Seeing Mark and seeing what new business shirt he was wearing was Dad's favourite part of the hospital visits.

I woke up in the afternoon a few days after the athletic banquet and was shocked to see Dixon and Jonah sitting there just chatting. My friends had made an executive decision to hang out at my house so that when I woke up I could be a part of their stories and friendship. Even if I slept and drooled like crazy, they would still be there just hanging out.

The feeling you get when you wake up to friends is indescribable. It makes you feel at first like, oh crap, I must have a drool puddle. Once that passes and you realize you do, but they are still there and still your friend, then you feel encompassed with love. It is the greatest feeling in the world, and I wish that each and every person in the world gets to feel so wanted, so included, so a part of something, and so loved.

This feeling really makes you re-prioritize everything. It makes you wonder why on earth you got mad over Dixon tripping you in the hall for a laugh, it makes you wonder why you felt left out when they didn't call you two years ago and they went to a movie without you because they still thought you were at a tournament. Friends showing this kind of support and love make you really value relationships. It makes me want to spend every second thanking them and just hanging out. It makes me wonder why on earth I got so stressed out about school and academics when really they are so much lower on the totem pole of importance.

Don't get me wrong, it's important to work hard and make something of yourself, or continue moving forward with your dreams and ambitions, but I used to feel like it was the end of the world if I got a bad grade on a quiz. There is more to life then the silly little things that consume our time or make us angry. I wanted nothing more than to just appreciate all the glory and positives in every single second of this life. I may not have been able to see out of both eyes yet, but I was definitely seeing the world more clearly than I had ever imagined before.

Magic

*Joy is what happens when
we allow ourselves to recognize
how good things really are.*

—Marianne Williamson

My life had become pretty repetitive and boring. My entertainment came from listening to people during my hospital visits and wondering what stories they had behind the little blip I had heard. One thing I have realized is that everybody you come into contact with—everybody in the whole world—has a story, a reason for what they are doing. I learned that it's not my place to judge, especially if I don't know what they are going through. I was inclined to learn as many people's stories as I could and just take a new appreciation for people and who they really are. People are so interesting, and we can learn so much if we just listen to what they say versus just hearing the words they speak.

I would still wake up every stinking hour for eye drops and I was getting pretty tired. One night I refused to roll over and let Mom put eye drops in. I thought I belonged to some one-eye tribe and she wasn't a part of it. I just kept repeating, 'Bring me to Chief Zoom Bah Bah; he will explain it to you.'

Sometimes when I went on my crazy Percocet dreams my brother and sister, Carter and Brianne, would just come sit in my room and watch. Once Carter even brought a bowl of popcorn and just sat there asking me questions to get the whacky responses I would come up with.

I had calmed down a little bit, when one evening I heard Miles at the door. He came up to my room where I was lying in bed. I had just woken up from a nap so I had quite a bit of energy. He came to the side of the bed, grabbed my hand, and said,

'Come on! I'm allowed to take you out for thirty minutes.'

I smiled uncontrollably at the thought of leaving my house for thirty minutes, especially with Miles. I hopped out of bed, realizing I was in boxers and a huge oversized T-shirt. One thing I had learned from this eye experience is that nobody really judges you or pays as much attention as you think to what you're wearing. I had become super comfy in my pajamas, and I was pretty sure that everybody that came to see me had seen me in them, as well as all of the hospital staff. I looked down through my squinted good eye, and Miles, anticipating what I was going to say, replied, 'Don't change—there is no time!'

I agreed, and we went running out the front door, or at least going as fast as I could move. Our hands were interlaced the whole time. Mom did eye drops right before he came so I was lucky to have the full thirty minutes free of my bedroom prison and my security guards known as the eye drops. He got my door for me and then ran to his side of the car, where he hopped in and started driving. It was night time so my eye wasn't too bothered by the light. Surprisingly the moon is still very bright, and even though my eye was closed with a patch on top, it was still irritated.

He drove the car all the way up the nearby ski hill, which I'm pretty sure is illegal. There was no snow, seeing as it was spring, and the hill was absolutely deserted. He got out of the car, opened my door, and led me to a blanket laid out with a bundle of flowers on it. There was also an I-pod set up with speakers. He took my hand and helped me sit down on the top of this hill (don't get me wrong, it's a hill, not a mountain, but it's still the highest point in my town). He turned the music on to some country slow beats even though he hates country, but he knew it was my favourite.

Then he handed me the flowers and looked me straight in my squinty good eye that I was struggling to keep open because I didn't want to miss a thing. He asked in a shaky nervous voice, 'Riley, would you be my date for prom?' He held his breath as I reached out and hugged him.

'Yes, of course!' I replied with my huge silly smile growing, even though it didn't seem possible for it to get any bigger.

Miles then explained why we were on the top of the ski hill. He said that he had brought me here because light has caused me so much pain in the past few weeks that he wanted me to see the beauty in it and remember how much I loved the sun. I just looked at him, confused, and then he put his fingers on my chin and turned my head so I was looking out over the city.

I could see the sparkling lights off in the distance, and even though it made my good eye water like crazy, it was a remarkable view that I couldn't believe. I turned back to Miles because looking at him was just as remarkable for me, and I said in barely a whisper, 'Thank you, thank you for everything'.

Then Miles stood up and turned the music up. We only had time for one song, but he asked me to dance up there on the top of the hill. He had to help me to my feet slowly because going from sitting to standing still hurt extremely bad. He basically held me up as we swayed back and forth to my favorite country slow song.

I hadn't known what perfect was before that moment. Apparently I stink at dreaming, because none of my dreams have ever been that good. Mom and Dad had been in on the plan, which is why we did eye drops right before he arrived. We arrived home and it was back to my bedroom prison, but I didn't mind one bit. Miles put me back to bed and tucked me in, then he left with a ridiculous smile on his face that must have been a twin to the one on my face as I fell asleep.

Mom came in right after he left; I thought it was for another set of eye drops, but really she just wanted all the details of my last thirty minutes. I told her how I still found it hard to breathe because Miles had literally made me that nervous. The butterflies were going crazy, and I told Mom that if I had had the energy at that moment, I would have been jumping and dancing on my bed like a little schoolgirl. Mom was living vicariously through me and all of my moments, even if there weren't many apart from her. Dad came in and asked what I had told the boy. He was trying to act like the tough guy Dad he's not. I told him that I said yes and he smiled at the sight of me being so happy. He left the room saying, 'Good. Miles is a respectable young boy, and I approve. I like how he asked my permission.'

In all reality I had no idea that Miles had asked my parents' permission because I was stuck in my room. I was just excited he had asked! I HAD A DATE TO PROM!!! I called Anabeth and she came over instantly. I replayed the events over and over again until I fell asleep mid-sentence.

I woke up hours later with Anabeth still at my bedside. I didn't even remember being woken up for hourly eye drops; I must have just woken up and then fallen right back to sleep.

I was for sure the luckiest girl in the world. Anabeth confirmed this fact when she said, 'I don't know why everybody feels sorry for you; you have a killer body for prom, you don't have to write exams or go to school, and you get to sleep all day . . . and now you have the number one bachelor boy at Billa-Aid taking you to prom!' I smiled at Anabeth's statement and was grateful for everything that had happened in the past weeks.

I was even grateful for that smoothie bottle exploding. I may have missed out on an OFSAA experience and my last few moments at Billa-Aid High School, but I had realized more important things. Like how amazing my family was and how I had a whole new set of priorities. The smoothie bottle explosion had shown me how much I impact other people's lives and who my true friends were. I don't wish that it never happened, I just wish that I could erase all the stress and pain I caused for other people.

Commencement

*Change is the essence of life.
Be willing to surrender who
you are for what you could become.*

The next few days went by very fast, but each moment went by very slow. It was like being trapped in a constantly sleepy tired state and not being able to break out. I was continuously weak and still wasn't eating very much, although I attempted to force some food down.

Commencement snuck up pretty fast. Before I knew it, I was supposed to be saying goodbye to Billa-Aid High School, all the teachers, and some friends that I didn't see outside of the building. My memories of being on sports teams, being a part of different clubs, and participating in music groups were all coming to an end. A huge part of my life had been over for weeks, but today it was ending forever. High school was done, and today we got to celebrate the new beginnings and successes we had experienced.

We drove to the building where the ceremony was being held. Mom came equipped with our handy-dandy lunch bag. Some of my eye drops had to be refrigerated so we brought icepacks and transported them in a pretty stylish lunch bag. It was the one thing I had control over, so I picked out a neat one with dinosaurs.

I had no idea what to expect or what I was supposed to do. I had been out of school for so long, the hustle and bustle felt new to me. I just stood among the chaos and then Jonah, Miles, Anabeth, and Dixon found me and got me into a gown. They helped me line up in the correct spot. All of my graduating classmates came up to me and gave me hugs and their supportive words. It was shocking to know how many people I had rooting for me. I just stood in line with my eyes closed, waiting for us to go in and begin the ceremony.

Mom snuck into the graduating class prep room and gave me some eye drops. The bustle and hustle became quiet, and I knew it was about to begin. Mom snuck back to her seat and then my line started moving and we were walking in. I was luckily behind Kelsey, who took very good care of me and held my hand once we started walking so both my eyes could remain closed. It was just too hard to keep my one good eye open, and it was watering like crazy.

I wore my yellow sandals so I wouldn't fall or trip, or at least it was less likely for me to trip than if I was wearing heals. The ceremony began and I almost instantly fell asleep. Then they introduced our valedictorian and I instantly woke up as they announced Kelsey. I was so proud of her and a little mad that she hadn't told me before, although my grounder boys had leaked out that it was one of my friends. I felt so honoured that I knew the person voted valedictorian.

I started to wonder who would receive the other awards, and I went through a bunch of my friends, feeling very special when I thought that a bunch of them would win some.

Kelsey went up to the middle of the stage to accept her award and address our graduating class with her speech. Her smile made the whole crowd melt, and I was so proud of everything she had done. She stepped up to the microphone and began by saying, 'I'd like to start by welcoming each and every lady and gentleman sitting in a blue gown here tonight. Each and every one of you has something to be hugely proud of. I would also like to thank and welcome all the individuals sitting at the front table and sitting dispersed between the blue gowns because, after all, without any of these lovely staff none of us would be here. Last, but not least, I want to thank and welcome all the other individuals that fill this auditorium: our parents, grandparents, sisters, brothers, friends, and all other supporters. Thank you for your continuous support, encouragement, and love for some of the hardest but best years of our lives!'

She went on, 'I am honored to be chosen to represent such an amazing group of people. All of you sitting in blue gowns are a part of what makes Billa-Aid so amazing. I see us all moving in unison towards our futures. We are all climbing up a huge mountain, with some intelligent and kind teachers belaying us every step of the way (supporting us with strong rope so we don't fall), with some steep slopes and tough bumps along the way . . . but always with the view of the top of the world and success in sight.

'Along our journey, with the help of teachers, parents, and friends, through the strength drawn from relationships and encouragement from all those around us, we have made it to this point. This is a life-changing moment for each and every one of us. We have climbed over those never ending bumps, we have shuffled across smooth rocks we never thought we could get over, and we learned a lot about the journey we had yet to venture.

'As a team we have reached the end of the mountain and soon will part ways. After one amazing endeavor, we sit and stare at the vast world, our future, and we should all feel the excitement as we are all about to embark on a brand new journey and move one step closer to realizing our hopes and dreams.

'With these new journeys that we are about to begin up new mountains and down different valleys, some farewells are in order. As graduates some of us will be moving out, moving away, and moving on—but the most important similarity that we all share is that we completed this chapter of our lives together and we are all moving forward with our lives.

'We are venturing out to explore the new spaces we can see from our mountain—to learn what independence truly means and to find not only happiness, but joy in whatever form it comes. We are setting out to establish ourselves as successful human beings and explore our interests. We take this step and are forced into a position to say goodbye to so many people who have become such important pieces of our lives. Yet, at the same time, we boldly place a foot one step closer to the person we will one day become. Each person we interacted with at this school has helped influence our lives and helped us become the person we will one day be. So as difficult and saddening as it may be, we must all say farewell to the school and community we have come to love over the past four, five years, or six years for you Mike. We are lucky we live in a generation with Facebook, MSN, cell phones, and every other piece of technology, because we will be able to stay connected to those who influenced our lives, even if it only means reading their updates on their home page.

'We're saying goodbye to a chapter in our lives that has yielded some of the best memories we've ever been blessed with. I look at all the events, groups, music, drama, and teams here at Billa-Aid, and I feel so happy to have experienced them all. Not just to be part of something, but to experience what it means to interact with such a fine group of young adults.

'We're moving on from a simple time in our life where we are able to compete against other teams with a jersey that we're proud to wear. Now we face components in the real world unmarked without a jersey. Being a part of that team has definitely left me with amazing memories, like our grad canoeing trip, or when Miles lost in ping-pong to the niner, when our teams won medals and trophies, and when relationships formed and changed our lives. I'll always remember everyone who has been a part of those smiles and giggles and times when I laughed so hard I peed my pants.

'I'll always remember our entire journey here, the relationships we've developed, not just the friends that have become family over the past four or five years, but the awesome teachers who have had such a great influence on us all. For four or five years, we've been taught by a group of adults who really care about our success. They are passionate, intelligent, and sincerely interested in us all.

'I'm sure none of us will forget Curly's crazy stories or any of the always-interesting science experiments. Each of us has our favourite moment and teacher who connected with us or who taught us something beyond what was taught in the curriculum. Those lectures and that love for teaching so many of our teachers exhibit has taught me that no matter where my life leads me, I should always pursue what I love. Being passionate about life and waking up excited every morning about getting to work is the path to a rich and successful life. The fact that every graduate in this room has learned so many life lessons in such a short period of time truly defines our time here as special.

She concluded, 'We have all matured together and experienced memories never to be forgotten. At this point we have all walked through those Billa-Aid doors for the last time as students, and now I hope you are all as excited as I am to begin this new chapter in our lives and walk through other doors as students. Now is the time to walk into our future!'

Kelsey's speech was amazing. She added in some songs and other funny stories from our four years at Billa-Aid. I was so proud she was my friend. She got a standing ovation, and then the ceremony continued.

I fell asleep and later on Kelsey had to wake me up to accept the greatest honour, the Principal's Prize. I had drool coming down my face when I got it, but it was such a surprise! It was awesome. I had no idea I would be remembered because I wasn't currently at the school attending classes. It had been hard listening to parts of Kelsey's speech because they were about memories I had missed out on. They were moments that could have defined somebody that I hadn't seen. Getting the Principal's Prize allowed me to be a member of Billa-Aid again, despite the fact that I was graduating. Receiving this award made me feel a part of something bigger than me; it made me feel like a part of my graduating class.

I almost tripped walking down from the stage after getting my plaque because I was still so weak and couldn't keep my good eye open. But just to hear the sound of clapping warmed my heart. People stood up and cheered, and I was in awe. People still remembered me.

After the grad ceremony, we all went out and took some pictures with our favourite teachers and friends. I had people coming up to me left and right. I had to sit down because I was so weak, but

I was able to be in many pictures with the flash off. The flash was way too bright and would hurt my eye.

After the endless pictures and hugs were over and people promised to get together in the summer, e-mail their favorite teacher, or come to visit, we all went to Brodie's to celebrate. I left early for bed because it was the longest I'd been up in a while, although going out gave Mom a break and a chance to have a nap. Anabeth came and protected me, along with my grounder boys and Miles. Anabeth was able to do my eye drops for me, and she was very precise and careful so I didn't need to worry something would go wrong.

It was so odd to see my friends outside of the hospital bed or my bed or couch at home. It was nice to see them and see that they still cared and treated me like a normal human. Even people that hadn't been to visit came over and asked genuine questions. It was absolutely amazing to see an individual's capacity to love somebody, and I was so joyful that I got to be the somebody to experience all the joy.

I had to leave pretty early, but it was still nice to pop in for a bit before I returned home to my bed, with my propped-up pillows and Mom as my official eye dropper. Turns out you can't escape the truth forever.

Time to Think

> *Like a comet blazing*
> *'cross the evening sky,*
> *gone too soon.*
>
> —MJ

The next few days were pretty lonely because people were finishing up last minute summer plans, classes, and prom preparation. High school students were all getting excited for freedom the following weekend after exams would be done. That's right, people were still studying for exams and stuff too. We have our commencement before so students are still around, and it's based on a projected mark and whether or not they think you will pass.

It's strange when you have nothing but time and your days still seem to go way too fast. Before the eye incident, I just lived my life for me, not needing to trust in anybody but myself. I would live minute to minute, trying to face each problem on my own, not seeing the bigger picture of the world out there.

Now I thought about the complexity of the world and the amazing and truly spectacular life there was. I had to give control and trust in something bigger then me, I had to trust in God to make it through the day. A lot of my minutes were spent praying and feeling completely at ease and comfortable despite my pain. It was incredible. I also realized my priorities had changed.

I no longer worried about school and grades and tests as much. Before the incident I would stress out and lose sleep over one quiz or one missed homework question. I sometimes got out of bed at 3 a.m. to complete a question I had forgot about during the evening because I couldn't sleep, knowing it wasn't done. School was a huge stressor, and I always compared myself to other people, especially my brother Carter. I also got so stressed out about the popular kids or the hidden curriculum; I would get really sad if I felt like somebody didn't like me, or if I might have upset somebody the previous day. I would sometimes feel bad for something that didn't even bother the person, like not seeing somebody in the hall and missing a chance to say hi. I would also get so stressed out about boys. Sometimes it felt like you were only somebody of value if you had a boyfriend by your side, and I definitely didn't.

Boys were a huge stressor for me. I would also have crushes on the boys that I didn't talk to or could never actually have a relationship with. I was afraid of commitment and being stuck with somebody forever. For some reason I thought that if I liked a boy and they liked me, I would have to marry him and be with him forever. For those reasons, I had unreachable standards. But yet I still yearned for that perfect boy that would get a check beside every perfect Prince Charming quality. This was very unrealistic, and by having the incident, I realized that boys aren't materials just like girls aren't. We can't manufacture the perfect Ken doll to be our boyfriend, and having a boy by your side doesn't make you any better or worse. I also realized that those quality lists we girls make go right out the window, because when you like that special boy, you get those butterflies down in your gut and that special feeling is most important, not those silly check marks. The last thing I learned about boys during this time is that when you are most comfortable and just being yourself is when you usually find the right boys. When I was myself with Miles, I got that butterfly feeling, and I wasn't even looking for a boy.

It's crazy what you learn when you have nothing but time to think. Sometimes I did wish my brain would turn off, though. I also realized that my number one priority was God, and my number two priority was my family. I hadn't realized how amazing they actually were and how important to my life they were. My family and friends moved up a lot in my priority list, and I realized that the relationships we make today will decide who we are Tomorrow. My friends and family honestly helped me through these times.

I also realized that no matter who you are or what you're doing, you are affecting somebody's life and you have the power to make somebody's day better. I realized that everybody has a story, and we just need to listen and learn as much from everybody that we can. I also learned that each individual is beautiful by his or her voices and that true beauty comes from the inside—even a blind person can pick up on it.

When you have nothing but time to think, you sure learn a lot. I was pretty bummed out that I had to miss all the excitement and end-of-the-year studying and parties. That's right, I was sad I couldn't study because it meant that I was out of that loop of stories and memories. I will never experience how hard Curly's study guide was for that final exam. Or how long that English exam was, or how that business exam was an insult to our intelligence. When you are missing out on something so simple as studying, you realize that there are little parts of it you enjoyed. I realized that there are positives in everything, like I found out I really enjoy complaining about studying and finals, I actually loved studying and the feeling you get once you have memorized or are able to apply and build upon a concept correctly. I even enjoyed the little songs I would sing at the top of my lungs to help me study. I missed these everyday moments and feelings when I was stuck in my vegetable state.

Prom was approaching faster than expected, and I spent a lot of my time daydreaming about my perfect night. Mom picked out my shoes and bag for me, and she also got the boutonnière or flower you pin on your date's jacket. I was set to go, but I still didn't feel a part of anything because I hadn't actually gotten out of bed. Oh well, my time to get out of bed was tomorrow, and I was super excited!

Prom

> *Dance till the stars come down*
> *From the rafters*
> *Dance, Dance, Dance till you drop.*
>
> —*W.H. Aude*

I slept for as long as possible in between drops to prepare for the big night. My prom wasn't going to be as fairytale perfect as I had dreamed, or not so much dreamed but witnessed on TV shows and movies. I went to get my hair done, and the girl that was doing my hair had heard about my story and told me she was praying for me. It was amazing how one story had touched people on the other side of town.

I got my hair done in this curly updo sort of thing. I had to trust the girl because I couldn't really decide for myself. I hadn't had time or the sight to look at pictures and pick out my own prom hairstyle. When she was done, I was really happy with it. I was happy just to have my hair in something other than the Chinese grandma bun I had been wearing for the past few weeks. I was already feeling more like a princess than I thought possible with my current eye-patch condition.

She asked if I was doing my makeup, but I told her I wasn't because I couldn't see and probably wouldn't trust my mother or sister getting close to my one good eye. Even though I could see out of my one good eye, I had no depth perception and would probably poke myself. You also can't do makeup on the eye if you have to close it; it just doesn't work. Good thing most people were used to me without makeup so it wouldn't be a shocker. I usually didn't wear makeup to school because of all the sports and sweating, plus it was too much of a hassle and I wanted every possible moment of sleep.

She asked if she could do my one good eye for me, and I was so excited! I told her I would love that. I envisioned my princess fairytale prom coming true. I hadn't had anyone really do my makeup before and I was really thrilled to see the results. She did my makeup with lots of eye watering because it was still so sensitive, even though it was my good eye. I was all dolled up, and I felt beautiful for the first time since the accident.

I was actually going to get to go to my prom, and I felt like a princess. I had an eye patch that matched my prom dress because we had to shorten my dress and we used the extra material for the patch. Mom ended up picking out a really cool pair of shoes that fit perfectly. I stood ready to go in the kitchen feeling like a princess and feeling like a normal grade twelve girl all at the same time. It was awesome.

When Miles arrived he had two different ties so he could see which would match best with the dress. We made our picks, and then I stuck the boutonniere on his coat jacket—or actually Mom did. I couldn't see and didn't want to stab him and have him bleeding all night, so Mom helped me out yet again. Miles presented me with a beautiful flower corsage. I love flowers and the significance of love demonstrated by somebody giving you flowers. I had dried the flowers my grounder boys and other family members had given me for my accident, and I planned to keep them forever. A warm butterfly excitement tingle shot up my body as Miles put the corsage around my wrist.

First we went into the backyard and took a bunch of pictures with just Miles and I. I loved that the pictures were an excuse for him to put his arm around me. It was so odd; I normally didn't like being touched and I appreciated my personal bubble, but for some reason it was different with Miles. I liked being in his arms.

I had to wear sunglasses over my eye patch because the light was still so painful to my eye. In most of the pictures my head was down because I couldn't stand holding my head up against the sun. I was energized strictly on excitement, and I knew it would be a long, hard night. I had my pain medication with me so I could last the night. Most of the time the only reason I remained standing for the pictures was because Miles was holding me up. Dad even pulled out the good old trusty saw and cut down a tree branch so that I could stand tall in the shade with less sun hitting my eye. This was a huge deal for Dad because he isn't the sort of handyman you see in some movies. He isn't the 'fixer-up' sort of dad. He fixes all of our problems that don't require manual labour, and while he often tries to fix the manual labour jobs around the house, they mainly result in a phone call to a company or a friend who can come over and help him fix things. Bringing out the saw was a huge step for Dad, and successfully sawing the branch down just showed the extreme measures my family was going to, all because of my eye.

We decided to stop by at Anabeth's house so we could take pictures with most of our graduating class. After about a bazillion pictures in my stylish sunglasses, we all sat down for some munchies. I still couldn't really eat, but it felt amazing just to be a part of my friends' company. I had missed out on this for so long. It was amazing to feel like a princess and be semi-normal for the moment.

A fire truck and a limo bus came to take some people to prom, but Miles and I just drove in Miles' Jeep in case I needed to come home. It was just another one of the many sacrifices Miles had made for me, and I loved him even more for it. He was so kind-hearted that he truly put my safety and health before his fun. I felt completely loved and wanted, and I never wanted this feeling to end.

We arrived at prom before everybody else, and Miles and I walked into the small castle that had been transformed into a dance area with our fingers interlaced. We walked out back and there was a beautiful pond with tables and tea lights flickering. Miles gave me some eye drops, and he asked me to dance.

I looked up at Miles with my one good eye with confusion. There wasn't even music on yet and nobody was there. Miles just looked down at me and said, 'I don't need music or anybody else to dance, all I need is you.'

I looked back up at Miles with that huge goofy smile that didn't seem to leave my face much that night. He led me to the dance floor, and I put my arms up around his neck. We began to sway back and forth, and I had to put my head on his shoulder because I was too weak to support it. It didn't matter, though; it felt like it belonged there. He put his arms around my now severely slender hips, and it was like we had become one. I loved the way he smelled and seemed to support me and all the problems in the world. I didn't have another thought in my head except for how perfect it was.

All of a sudden the DJ came in and started up the song 'Stealing Cinderella' by Chuck Wicks. My perfect moment just got even better. With both my eyes closed by choice, I couldn't help but let all the pain I had had bottled up go, and tears started slowly dripping down my one good eye's cheek. Miles was my Prince Charming and I loved dancing with him.

Way too soon, the song came to an end and more people started trickling in. I had to go sit down because I was way too weak to stand after dancing. The music picked up and all our friends arrived. Everybody was dancing, but I was too weak to dance to the fast songs, and I hardly had energy to sway for the slow songs. Miles did eye drops for me every half hour, and Anabeth helped out as well. My friends are truly angels.

I just wanted to be surrounded by all the people I loved, and I was. I felt minimal pain because I was high on Percocets and the love that was surrounding me. I guess we were all the same that night at prom. Nobody had their labels, because it was the last time we would be together as a class. We were all equal because we were all starting new beginnings. Everybody hugged everybody. Some people came to prom high on the thought that school at Billa-Aid was over, some people came to prom excited to dance, others came with the liquid courage known as alcohol. And me, I was excited too. I wasn't buzzed on alcohol, but I was buzzed on my pain medication and the life I had.

I felt horrible for Miles; I was probably the worst date ever. I could hardly dance, I needed eye drops every thirty minutes, I laughed at everything (because of the pain meds), and I wanted to talk to everybody! Miles came to me sitting outside by the pond with the twinkle tea lights, and he took my hands in his. He stared right into my good eye. Did you know that when you look at somebody, you only look at one eye at a time? So right there in that moment when Miles chose to look me in the eye that was normal, he choose to make me feel loved, to feel normal. He chose to make that moment the best moment ever. He asked if I felt up for a dance. I looked back at those loving eyes and choked on my words as I replied that I really didn't have the energy to stand.

Miles just looked back with his sly smile and said, 'Who says you need to be able to stand to dance?'

I was confused, but my confusion was soon cleared as he swooped me up in his arms and headed to the dance floor. Miles carried me in his arms like a little child and danced with me like a little doll. I had my arms wrapped around his neck and that goofy smile on my face again. Miles had done it again. He surprised me and took my pain and worries away. He made me feel normal—well, at least like I wasn't missing out on anything. We danced the night away and took much needed breaks for eye drops, but I didn't miss out on anything as our friends danced with us and Miles carried me song after song. It was like magic!

The DJ came on the speaker announcing the last song and the end to our high school days. The end of some friendships, the end of Billa-Aid classes, the end of sports, and the end of perfect moments. The last slow song came on and Miles and I just held each other as I looked up at his beautiful face. He carried me to the pond as the song was coming to an end, and he leaned down and kissed me on the cheek. As his hands brushed against my face, the butterflies in my stomach were doing flips!

I looked up at him and asked, 'Did you miss?' with a sly smile on my face.

Miles just laughed and leaned in and kissed me on the lips. It was the softest, most perfect kiss ever known to humans. Our lips parted, as did our moment when people came crowding out of the castle and into the courtyard. They asked if we were going to go to Anabeth's for a campfire.

We both nodded and got up to leave our prom. The grounder boys came with us in Miles's Jeep, and we stopped at each of their houses to pick up sweatpants and let their parents know where we were going, if they were still up. The grounder boys and Miles all live on the same street, so Miles parked at Dixon's house, which was in the middle of them all, and they all split to get changed. Dixon's little brother was outside playing basketball.

I decided to get out of the car and see if I had any pieces of my old identity left. He passed me the basketball and I tried dribbling. It felt different, not as comfortable as before. Before the accident, basketball and sports was who I was but now I had so much more to me. Dixon's little brother and I took some shots and goofed around, and soon the boys had returned to witness the hilarious sight of a half blind girl all jazzed up looking like a princess in a prom dress, attempting to play basketball on the driveway under the starlight and one porch light. We all laughed a laugh full of joy and loaded the Jeep to be off to spend every minute of our prom night together.

When we arrived at Anabeth's, the campfire was already blazing and people were everywhere. I was tired and we all just laid down on blankets around the fire and looked up at the stars. Some people started playing the guitar, others roasted marshmallows, but we were all together and so comfortable with each other. Some of our graduating class left Anabeth's and relied on other things and other substances to have fun.

I realized through this whole thing that I never want to lose control of my body again, and I will never put myself in a position where that could happen with those kinds of substances. I lost control of my body once by being put on medication and forced to be so weak; even my happy pills altered my realization of what was going on around me. I never wanted to consciously lose control of my body if I had any say in the matter. I usually wanted to be in control of my decisions and actions in my life. The trauma helped me realize I also wanted to be in control of my body if I had that choice.

I was so exhausted that I just laid there on the blankets with all my friends surrounding me and dozed in and out of the conversations. It was a perfect end to a perfect night. The night felt like a dream, but one where I was safe and protected. That's what friends do for you, they protect you. I got home at 6 a.m. because Miles woke me up and said that we should probably go home. He had been texting my mom and giving her updates, assuring her I was still getting my eye drops and that I was okay. After my fairytale prom, I was forced back to my state of sleeping and eye drops and not eating for many days just to recover and gain some energy. Prom had wiped me weak, but I was filled with memories and moments I will never forget.

Change

> *It is one of the blessings of old friends
> that you can afford
> to be stupid with them.*
>
> —Ralph Waldo Emerson

After prom, my friends would stop by for a last minute hangout before their summer adventures began and they moved on to the next chapter of their lives. Dixon and Jonah told me about the pranks that Brodie and some of the hockey players pulled in the last few days of school. Hearing about how there were pigs let loose in the school cafeteria and a major food fight days ago made me realize how abstract and distant those last few days of high school really were for me.

It made me realize how much of my life I had actually missed out on. I was exhausted from prom and acquaintances' visits were kept short. I didn't realize it would be the last time I would see some of these people. They moved on to their summer dreams of camp jobs, tree planting somewhere up north, or traveling the world before they became too in debt from university. Kelsey went to work up at her favourite summer camp, and I knew I wouldn't be hearing from her for the rest of the summer—camp life was busy, with hardly enough time to sleep. I was beginning to become a part of my friends' high school memories, left in the past while they went on living their futures.

Once I had caught up on my sleep, I was into a new, different routine. I still continued with the eye drops and the doctor's appointments, but now I felt I was so close to climbing the peak of the mountain and just scaling my way down the other side. The top of the mountain was now in sight, and with the goal in hand, I had more energy for the climb. The pain became secondary, partially because I was so used to it, but also because I realized that I needed to focus on other things. Anabeth, Brianne, and I would hang out all day long and listen to our favourite television shows. They sacrificed the beautiful days outside just to spend time with me.

Miles came over eight days after prom and I was finally gaining a little bit of energy, enough to sit up and talk to people for longer than five minutes. I was slightly worried that I hadn't heard from Miles in a few days. Normally he would bring his Mom's famous cookies over or we would just hang out together every single day. Miles' Dad was never mentioned. His Dad had walked out on their family when Miles was four, and they had never spoken since. Miles had brought him up a few times the past week and I think he was more curious about his father now that he was older.

Miles came in and joined me on the couch where I made my home the past months. He sat down and held my hand, but something was wrong. He wasn't smiling, and it looked like it pained him to be there. He didn't make eye contact as he started talking.

'Riley, I have been putting off telling you this for a little while because I didn't want to add any more pain into your life.'

I hated when people built up what they were going to say before they said it. It's like, okay Riley here is something really bad I'm going to tell you, and I want you to prepare for it. Well, you know what I do instead of preparing for what you're going to tell me? I play worst case scenario in my head, I think your dog died, or you didn't actually graduate and you're going to have to go back another year, or maybe even that we are breaking up. Miles went on to tell me,

'Riley, I decided which university I was going to go to and I sent back my letter of acceptance.'

I did find it odd that we hadn't talked about that yet, but I just figured he didn't want to talk about something that I could potentially never get to do. I thought he was preventing hurting my feelings by not talking about the parts of his life that I could not be a part of or experience on my own yet.

'I am going to the University of British Columbia next year, Riley.'

He waited as this information sunk in. University of British Columbia. That was on the other side of the country; that wasn't just a few hours' drive to hang out for the weekend, that was a buckle-your-seatbelts-and-put-your-seats-to-their-up-right-position-get-ready-for-a-flight.

'Wow, that's pretty far,' I replied. I figured seeing this as a factual decision would probably be best right now.

Miles knew how much this decision had hurt me. It also hurt him that he would be so far away, but I was happy he had made the best decision for him. The program and experience he would have there was the best fit for Miles. It was also where Miles' father lived, and I thought maybe he wanted to rekindle that relationship. I hated how sometimes you are supposed to be happy for somebody, and maybe you actually are happy for them, but you still felt so awful, like your lungs just got tighter and there is a huge lump in your stomach.

We both kind of just took what he had said and digested it for a minute, and then we continued on acting as though he had just told me an update in the weather; we acted as though it was sunny with not a cloud in sight when really a tornado was coming.

Once Miles left, I realized I had to start sorting out my university plans if they were actually going to work out. I called the university and talked to them about my situation, asking if I would be able to get my money back if I wasn't able to go. The doctors had told me I shouldn't even be applying. I had no idea if I would ever get to go to university and fulfill those dreams I had about becoming a doctor, marine biologist, sports announcer, teacher, or whatever other profession excited me that day.

I had realized throughout the whole eye experience so far that I was really not as blind as everybody thought I was. Sure, I was literally blind, but my life had become so much clearer than before. Before the accident I was more blind to life than I was now. Now I was only unable to see shapes and colours. Before the accident I didn't know who I was aside from my athletic identity, I didn't know how important my friends and family were, I didn't realize how prayer and a change in attitude can totally change your physical strength for the day. I had no idea about how the decisions I made influenced the people and the world around me. I knew I had lots of Facebook friends, but I couldn't imagine impacting or influencing any of their lives by simply smiling down the hallway at school or holding a door open for somebody. I was no longer blind to the bigger world outside of my life. Before the accident, I had a blind perspective when I woke up each morning to face life, but now I was free and had so much more insight about how the world worked and how important each individual was that was living in it. I might be physically blind now, but I could see more clearly than ever. I could see the things that mattered and the things that would always matter.

I knew that my family was always going to be there for me no matter how annoying Brianne got or how angry I was with my Mom when she wouldn't let me go out for a night. I also realized that every second of every day matters and that each decision we make affects somebody. My world had grown by this experience, and I was no longer stuck seeing the world for my problems and my bad tests that made it come crashing down. I was beginning to see the world outside of me and realize that there were people a plane ride away who were just happy to survive another day with food, or to get the opportunity to study. I was realizing that, although my eye was blind, I still had sound, touch, taste, and movement to enjoy. The world was a beautiful place, and I had taken it for granted for too long. I was becoming an individual with my own morals and priorities that nobody could change. I had my family, and no matter what happened with my eye, I would get through it because no amount of pain can ever take away the love you are surrounded with, no pain can ever let you forget that there is somebody holding your hand and helping carry that pain for you.

After Miles left and my butterflies had simmered down a little bit, I started to second-guess me and him together. Sure, I knew that I loved him and he made me a better person and truly cared for me, but I felt like I was holding him back from his own realizations and experiences. Plus, just like not knowing his Dad or the whole experience surrounding his Dad, there was a lot I did not know about him yet. I pushed those thoughts away and focused on our perfect prom, and the way he took my breath away by just being in the same room as me. I pushed those other thoughts away for now.

Goodbye

*How lucky am I to have people in my life
that are hard to say goodbye to*

Anabeth came over the next day and asked me some serious questions I hadn't considered before. She was researching the smoothie company and asked me if I had ever considered suing them. I looked at her and just laughed in bewilderment. I told her I would never consider such a thing and would only sue them if it meant preventing other people from getting harmed or hurt. I didn't want anybody to have to go through what I went through, even though there were lots of good things that came out of it. Nobody deserved that pain.

We dropped the issue and never looked back; we continued watching our favourite television show and giggled all day long. Mom would come in and give me eye drops. Pretty soon Anabeth had organized her work schedule on the days I had appointments in Toronto so that when I was gone visiting the hospital she was working.

It was strange with summer starting and people leaving. Not being able to go up to the camp I was supposed to work at for the whole summer was one of the hardest things ever. I knew how amazing Muskoka Woods was and I wanted to go so bad, but I just wasn't allowed to leave my new home on the couch with Mom doing eye drops what felt like every second. Plus, I still had to go to the hospital all the time. It was like a medical marvel; doctors came from all over to look at the fungus in my eye.

A week after Miles and I had our University of British Columbia chat he came over for a visit, and I knew something was wrong. He had been very distant. He came right into the living room and my couch, and he looked me in the eyes. He had tears forming, and he began the toughest conversation we had ever shared together.

He began by telling me how amazing I was and how I had impacted his life, and that was when I knew I was in trouble. Why would he be tearing up if he was just talking to me and telling me how perfect I was in his eyes? He then told me that he thought I was the girl he wanted to marry and spend the rest of his life with, but he could not be my boyfriend right now. He could not date me and hold me back from whatever I had next in my life. He had to move forward and experience university with all it had to offer. He wanted to leave me behind, and I was now a burden to him.

His words stunned me and stopped those butterflies right in their tracks. He was breaking up with me. Miles was leaving me behind. I was being dumped. This boy who had given me hope when I had very little, this boy who helped me get excited for the next day even if it was filled with pain, was leaving me in his past. I would just be a distant memory of some girl he once knew.

Miles was moving on, not to another girl, but to other possibilities and activities I might never get to participate in. I was stuck on my living room couch with my stupid eye patch and lousy eye dropper, and he was out experiencing the world. I just tied myself together with a smile and said that I understood. I couldn't hold him back forever, and I thanked him for helping me through some of the toughest days of my life. I waited to fall apart until he was gone. I think I resorted to my old ways of pretending everything was okay and just smiling to cover up the pain.

When he left, he kissed me on the forehead and said goodbye for now, but it felt like goodbye forever. As soon as he left, I curled up in a ball on my couch and cried under the blanket. It stung my eye, but the tears just kept coming. It felt like I was a waterfall that had just been opened. Water was pouring out of me, with my body shaking violently, and nothing I could do would stop it. It was a different type of pain that took hold of my body. This pain was the pain of being left out. The pain of being built up then broken down. It was the pain of Miles leaving me behind. I wanted to disappear and hide under the covers never to be found again. It was so different from when Miles and I first started liking each other; then, I just wanted to be noticed and be the only thing that appeared in his world.

After I wallowed in my self-pity for a few days I finally let Anabeth come over. We talked about how stupid Miles was, but I knew I couldn't even pretend to be mad at him. When you like somebody, you're blinded by all their imperfections, and I still had Miles up on a pedestal that was out of my reach.

Anabeth helped me realize all the new perspectives that the eye incident had taught me, and I slowly got used to the idea of being single, or not being Miles' girlfriend. I was a strong individual, and I had no idea what would be happening in my life in the next few days, let alone years. It just reminded me that I had to be thankful for all the moments and love shared with my friends while I can. I would still think about Miles and look at prom pictures, but as the days in the summer months passed and I would visit the doctors, new hope blossomed in my life and new possibilities were just around the corner.

Shock

> *Be kind,*
> *for everyone you meet*
> *is fighting a*
> *hard battle*
>
> —Plato

Carter came sprinting down the stairs one day and stood right in between Brianne, Anabeth, and I. He looked at me and basically spit out his next sentence. 'Do you know who owns the banana strawberry smoothie company?'

I was like, 'Carter, what are you talking about?'

'The company. The company who owns the smoothie that cut your eye open? Do you know who owns it?!?!'

I just stared at him with a face that I often showed Carter, which meant what relevance does this have to my life now? I thought we had moved past that.

'No, Carter I have no idea, who is it?'

'MILES' DAD!!!!!'

My jaw dropped. I was in utter shock. The little Lego pieces in my head were coming together—Miles my ex-boyfriend who I still loved, but who had just dumped me, Miles. His father was the one who sold the product, the smoothie bottle that cut my eye in half. Miles' father was responsible for some of what had happened? Was there somebody to blame? Could I finally be mad at Miles for breaking my heart and his father for ruining my high school career?

Carter showed me the facts and the names, and it was true. Miles' father was the owner of the company who invented and sold those banana strawberry smoothies. Should I tell Miles? He doesn't even talk to his father, but I hadn't talked to him in the last three days.

I decided I would call Miles and tell him just so he would be aware, plus I needed to come to terms that Miles was leaving. Just as I decided to pick up the phone, the doorbell rang. Carter answered the door and led Miles into the living room. I put down the phone. Miles was a mess.

'Riley, I know we have to break up because our lives are leading us in different directions right now, but I just wanted to tell you that I have never stopped loving you and I never will.' Miles looked at the floor as he finished his sentence.

I was in complete shock; how was I supposed to just let somebody that I loved disappear out of my life? I told him that we would stay in touch. When we were ready and in the same place in life, maybe we would get back together and last a lifetime.

Just maybe our cards would line up and we would be able to grow old together. I told him that there was still hope; this wasn't goodbye, but more of a halftime and break. I needed him to let me grow and get better so that when we came back together, we would both be the best we could be. That way, by being together, we'd help each other be better. This was a totally different mindset to leaving one another. This meant we could still text each other and stay connected throughout the year. It just meant we didn't need to be sad about the distance, but instead we could be excited for when we would see each other next.

Then I looked at Miles and told him that I had some other information I had to tell him. I swallowed a big gulp of air and told him that his father was the owner of the smoothie company. Miles' face dropped and all the built-up anger he had for his father came rushing through his veins.

'My father hurt the most important people in my life! First he hurt my mother and my family and now, now he hurt you!' Then Miles punched the pillows that I was sitting next to so hard that I tensed in fear. He took a few seconds to think about his new current situation, then continued talking. 'When I go to university in British Columbia and I see my father, I'll show him a piece of my mind! I'll show him what it feels like to have the ones you love hurt so deeply with nothing you can do to take that pain for them. I'll show him.' Then Miles just stood silent in thought for a few minutes, and his face began to calm.

I then spoke up, terrified I would start another rampage. 'Miles, it wasn't your Dad's fault. He didn't know that this would happen; he was just doing his job, you can't blame him for this. Plus there are lots of good things that have happened; just think we may not have become this close if there wasn't a reason for you to visit every day to see how I was doing. We may not have had the best memory in the world at prom or on top of the ski hill. You should give your Dad a chance, a chance to explain his story and the reasons behind what happened to your family. This year is going to be a great chance for you to see a different side of your father than the side you imagined so you could get angry at someone. He may be a better man than you thought.' I finished and held my hands tight, trying to read Miles' expression to see how he would handle these ideas.

He responded that he was going to give his father a chance, but that didn't change how mad he had made him and how his father would hear about all the pain that he caused. I think that Miles was excited to meet his father and see if his father could be somebody he could look up to in the future instead of look to blame for all of his problems.

Miles decided to stay for the rest of the afternoon, and Anabeth came over to see for herself if his intentions were true and loyal. After Anabeth quizzed Miles endlessly over the recent break up and decided that he actually had both of our best interests at heart, we all hung out the rest of the day. We even decided that I was going to attempt to go into the pool. It was a gorgeous day outside, but there were clouds so it wasn't too bright. I had an eye patch and multiple sunglasses and goggles covering my eyes. Then Miles opened the door to the backyard and shaded me from the sun with a towel so it wouldn't hurt too bad. I continued to walk with Miles and Anabeth's guidance to the edge of the pool. I was able to put my feet in and walk in the shallow end. My eye burned, but the feeling of the fresh pool water and the summer air was well worth the pain! I had waited so long to be outside it was magnificent. There was no splashing or shenanigans because I wasn't allowed to get my eye wet, but just the fact that I was in the water and it wasn't a gross bathtub made me very happy.

After the crazy events of our day came to a close and Miles and Anabeth went home for the night, I had time to think through some things. I felt extremely happy that Miles and I were still in love and loyal to one another, but I did know we would be apart this next year. It would be good to allow us to grow individually, but it would be tough because we would miss each other. Being apart just gave us more to talk about, and we would find exciting new ways to communicate with one another.

Epilogue—Triumph over tragedy

Now I am currently sitting on the dock in my yellow polka dot bathing suit at Muskoka Woods. My eyes are both closed and I'm enjoying the sun beating down on me without immense pain. I cannot see out of my right eye, but the doctors are working on it and I'm scheduled for surgery in two weeks. My right eye can open sometimes when it's not so bright, and I almost pass for an individual with two healthy eyes. When I go outside or somewhere bright, my right eye closes instinctively, giving me my camp name Wink, because it looks like I'm winking.

Today I'm not fully recovered and I don't know if I'll ever see out of my right eye again, or maybe even lose sight in both eyes because of sympathetic reasons, but I have overcome the initial tragedy and realized that there is always hope. No matter the situation, there is some hope that we can hold onto and help us get through today's tragedy and move onto tomorrow's miracle.

Triumph over tragedy and moving forward have helped me be allowed to be a volunteer for a week up at Muskoka Woods. I know that life isn't working out the way I planned—I didn't plan to have a smoothie lid slice my eye in half—but I do know that life is full of miracles. Each moment can bring hope and happiness, even if there is tragedy.

So I'm here at Muskoka Woods with Anabeth sitting at the docks beside me doing drops for me. I don't have to do them as frequently and I have enjoyed getting two hours of sleep in a row. I love being surrounded by nature and the interesting people Muskoka Woods brings together. There are lots of international staff, and Anabeth and I sometimes speak with a British accent just because it catches on. Anabeth can make the most simple things in life glorious. She truly sees how each day can be an adventure with exciting twists and positive outcomes. I am only allowed to be away from doctors for one week, so I am soaking up all the Muskoka Woods love possible while I am here.

Miles is out in British Columbia with his father. Turns out he is a pretty interesting man with lots of neat stories. They were going rock climbing together today and sailing tomorrow. Miles writes me a letter every day and we Skype twice a week. I miss him terribly but love his letters. I cannot wait until I get to see him again.

I have gotten stronger every day since the accident, even in the persistent face of adversity. I plan to go to university in the fall and stay in residence. I do plan for tomorrow, because even if life doesn't always go as planned, if I have a chance,

I am going to try and take every chance I get, plan for the most exciting and fun moments, and live my life for all I can.

I realize that I have no control about whether I will actually medically be able to go to university in the fall, I have no control about if my eye is going to get better within the next five years, or if I will ever see again, I don't know how many surgeries I have left before I stop seeing the doctors, I have no idea who my friends will be in the future, and I have no idea if I will love Miles forever or just have times when I will be in love with him (like right now). But what I do know is that we do have control over some decisions and moments, and these are the moments I no longer waste. I do have control about my new perspective and my future and what I am going to do with it. I am not a normal person with a normal story, but nobody is. Each person in this world has had experiences that shape who they are today. I am no longer normal, and I am no longer living with a blind perspective.

About the Author

I was born in Kitchener Ontario and have lived in Kitchener throughout my childhood. I grew up with my older brother, younger sister and loving parents. I am currently attending Brock University in St. Catherines. I live away from my family in a house in St. Catherines throughout the school months. I love reading books and until two years ago had never considered actually writing a book to be read by others. I recently experienced a trauma and had many changed perspectives that I believe deserve to be shared with the world. This book is written in the hopes to inspire individuals and show everybody who reads it the importance in their own story. This book also allows a trauma to shine in a positive light. My hope is to allow this book to inspire and allow the readers to feel the support and love of their current community. I hope that this book allows individuals to escape their current realities and travel to an enchanting new world that may change their outlook of their current situation.